THE
A
X

The AX
Copyright © 2023 by Jeanette J Kossuth-McAdoo

Published in the United States of America
ISBN   Paperback: 979-8-89091-370-8
ISBN   eBook: 979-8-89091-371-5

All rights reserved. No part of this publication may be reproduced, stored in a retrieval system or transmitted in any way by any means, electronic, mechanical, photocopy, recording or otherwise without the prior permission of the author except as provided by USA copyright law.

The opinions expressed by the author are not necessarily those of ReadersMagnet, LLC.

ReadersMagnet, LLC
10620 Treena Street, Suite 230 | San Diego, California, 92131 USA
1. 619. 354. 2643 | www.readersmagnet.com

Book design copyright © 2023 by ReadersMagnet, LLC. All rights reserved.

Cover design by Ericka Obando
Interior design by Daniel Lopez

THE AX

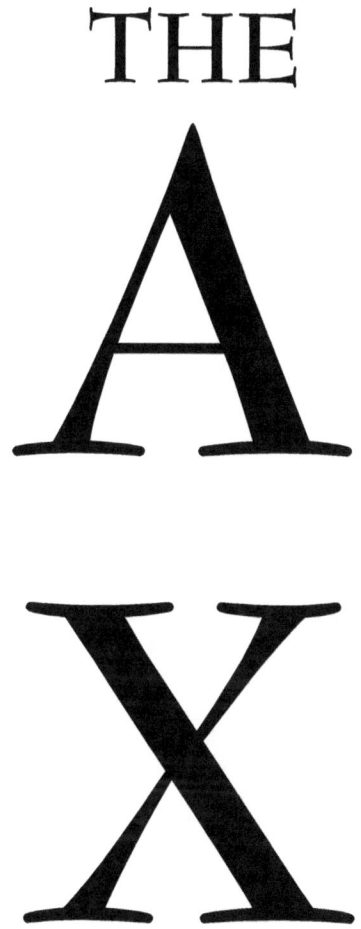

JEANETTE J KOSSUTH-MCADOO

CONTENTS

Chapter 1 11
Chapter 2 37
Chapter 3 65
Chapter 4 92
    BACK OFF 92

Chapter 5 109
    STAY OUT OF THIS 119
    THIS IS YOUR LAST CHANCE, BACK OFF 123
    YOU'RE RESPONSIBLE 124
    YOU WILL DIE 128
    YOU'RE RUNNING SHORT OF TIME 137
    THIS IS YOUR FINAL WARNING, BACK OFF 138
    YOU MUST DIE, DEVIL 144
    CONTINUE AND YOU WILL DIE 149

Chapter 6 153
    "LIAR" 161
    PAUL DEVIL 165

My name is Jeanette J. McAdoo and I was born and raised in McKeesport Pa. It has always been my secret passion to someday write books and now I am. I still live in Pa and get a great deal of encouragement from family and friends. Hope you will enjoy this book as much as I did writing this. A friend's son inspired me on this one.

I dedicate this to Brandon Lipani who inspired me to write this book. Thank you Brandon, and also to your parents, Johanna and Tom Lipani, for their contribution.

I would like to thank Nicole Campbell of nikol_decay on Instagram for consenting to let me use one of her photos for the cover of my book. Thank you.

-Jeanette

A peaceful town has been turned upside down when a string of murders is being committed with an ax. Not even the police can figure out a motive. There is no rhyme or reason about the murders or who is committing them, not even a connection in some way with the victims: When Dr. Lewis Tanner arrives back in town after being out of the country for a while, he studies each case and believes he knows whom the murderer is, but how can he?

THE AX

CHAPTER 1

Paula Lived woke up to a beautiful sunny morning, showered, dressed and put on a pot of coffee. She turned on the television while she made breakfast; a news bulletin was being broadcast that caught Paula's attention.

"Late last night a local man had reported to police a suspicious person lurking around the neighborhood. After the police arrived and did an investigation; they found the body of a man in his home. Police say the man's name was Bill.

Deerfield. We'll have more information in the next update."

Paula grew numb with great disbelief. There had to be a mistake! Everyone loved Bill. Quickly she dialed his number in hopes he would answer and put an end to this nonsense. After two rings she heard a male voice on the other end.

"Bill! Bill! Is this really you? The news broadcaster said you were dead!"

The voice on the other end wanted to know whom he was speaking with.

"Bill, it's me, Paula!

"Miss, this is Lieutenant James Garrett. May I ask your last name?

Paula hung up and fell to the floor in tears. Her chest felt heavy and she was scared. Pain tore through her body as she screamed out Bill's name. Tears streamed down her face and she could barely breath. This just had to be a nightmare.

"Oh please, God! This can't be true, please!"

Her fists pounding on the floor in anger, briefly she raised her head to see her friend Rebecca standing in the doorway. Paula never heard her come in.

"Rebecca, did you hear the news? They're wrong, they have to be."

Rebecca rushed to Paula's side, holding her and trying to comfort her, feeling her pain. She would have done anything to spare her of this tragedy. After about thirty minutes of crying, Rebecca helped Paula off the floor and into the living room to rest. After putting on water for tea, Rebecca made a couple of phone calls. She carried the tea in to Paula and wrapped a blanket around her shoulders. Then she gently stroked the side of Paula's face with the back of her hand, gently wiping the tears from her face.

"Carefully sip your tea, it's very hot."

Paula never acknowledged her, she seemed to be somewhere else but not in this room. Maybe she was thinking about the times she spent with Bill. They shared many wonderful times together; they were even planning for their wedding. Now Paula was robbed of her life with Bill.

"Paula! Honey, listen to me. I called your boss Mr. Langdon and he sends his sympathies. He said if there is anything he can do, don't hesitate to call. I'm here for you as long as you need me. I want to help you through this."

There was a knock at the door and Rebecca went to see who was there.

"Hello, I'm Lieutenant Garrett. I'm working on the investigation of Bill Deerfield's murder. A call came through this morning while we were there. We traced the phone number to this residence. I'd like to talk to you if I may?"

"I suppose it would be alright, please come in. My name is Rebecca. My friend lives here, her name is Paula. She is… was Bill's fiancé. Most likely she called to see if what she heard on the news this morning was the truth. You must have verified that for her."

"I'm very sorry, really I am. May I speak with her?"

"If you can, she's right there. She seems to be in some sort of daze from all this."

Lieutenant Garrett saw Paula in the living room; it was plain to see she was very disheveled. This was the part of his job he detested most, but it is part of the job.

"Are you sure you can't wait to talk to her, she is very upset and shaken. I can't imagine her being of any use to you in this condition."

"I'm very sorry, but I do have to question her now. She may know something and not realize it, so we try and jog the memory."

"Come in officer, my name is Paula. Do you know who would do this? Or why?"

"We don't know anything yet. I was hoping there would be something you could help me with."

"I can't imagine what, but go on and ask your questions."

They talked a while, but neither had anything to say to help the other.

"Lieutenant, Bill was a well-known man in this town. Everyone loved him. To the best to my knowledge, no one would want to harm him."

Once again she burst into tears and James turned and apologized for upsetting her.

"Lieutenant, would it be alright for me to make his final arrangements?"

"I don't see why not. I'll call and let you know when we're ready to release the body. There, of course, will be an autopsy."

Rebecca showed the Lieutenant his way out, then went to get some aspirin and water for Paula. She did everything she could to keep her calm, but of course that was not an easy task. Not even Rebecca could believe what happened to

Bill. The person who did this would have to be a monster. This day was very long and dusk was setting. Paula was uneasy the entire day, so Rebecca gave her a sleeping pill so she could rest. She waited for Paula to fall asleep before she turned in for the night. The night was long. She could hear Paula crying and wanted to console her, but she knew she would need some time to let it out in her own way. It was the toughest thing Rebecca has ever done. It tore her apart leaving her like that, but she had to give her time. According to the clock on the wall, it was one thirty in the morning when Paula finally went to sleep.

The next day Rebecca was up early, made breakfast, and had a list made to help Paula get done everything she needed. The aroma from the cooking is what woke Paula. She walked in the kitchen, finding Rebecca at the stove.

"Rebecca, it's sweet of you to want to help me, but I can't ask you to take off work for me. I don't want to cause you any trouble."

"Don't worry, my boss understands and he gave me as much time as I need. I'm here for you. I want to help. Now while I finish getting breakfast, why don't you look over this list and make sure it's complete."

While Rebecca poured the coffee, Paula carefully looked over everything she had on the list. Everything seemed to have been covered, at least as far as she could tell for now.

"I'm afraid I wasn't much help to that policeman yesterday."

"I'm sure he knows you did your best. You told the truth, what more could he ask for?"

"Do you think he suspects me of hiding something… or something?"

"Of course not! I'm sure he just thought there may have been something you could have told him that would help him catch the killer."

"What could that possibly be?"

"I wish I could say I knew. Maybe an argument he had with someone, who knows. Listen, don't put yourself out thinking about it, you have enough to deal with. Relax and enjoy your breakfast."

Paula hugged Rebecca. They sat down together to plan the day. As far as she could tell, the list was complete. All she had to do was the toughest part, begin the arrangements. She wasn't sure it was sinking in yet, but at some point it will. The sooner they finished this list the better. The agony was stressful enough; Paula just wanted this to be over with. Not that she wanted to forget Bill, just the pain she is feeling. The funeral director told them he could have the work done as soon as the police release the body. A small ceremony would be scheduled for everyone to say his or her final goodbye.

"Thank you so much! I do appreciate the expeditious manner for this situation. This is a difficult time for all involved."

"Believe me, Miss Lived, I do understand. Would you like us to dispose of the ashes for you?"

"Actually, no thank you, I'll be taking care of that personally. Thank you so much. You've been extremely helpful."

Rebecca had a concerned look on her face. She couldn't figure out why Paula wouldn't let the director dispose of the ashes. After leaving the funeral home, Rebecca had questioned Paula's judgment for disposing of the ashes.

"Paula, are you sure you don't want the funeral director to handle that for you? I know how difficult this has to be for you."

"I'm sure. Bill use to hunt whenever he could, near the Verde River. He uses to talk about how beautiful it was there. His last trip there, he brought home a quail and cooked dinner for me. He always looked forward to those trips and he enjoyed them immensely. He talked about it all the time. It seems only appropriate to scatter his ashes in a place where he found such enjoyment."

"Well, I suppose if you feel that strongly about it, whatever you want. I'm here for you, you know that. I just want to make this as easy as I can."

"I know that, and I do appreciate everything you're doing, I can't thank you enough."

"We're almost through with this list. How would you feel about going out? to dinner, my treat."

"Thanks, but I'm really not very hungry. I have plenty to eat at my place, we can go there. You can have whatever you like."

"You have to eat something, even a little. You'll need your strength."

"I'll have something, I promise."

Rebecca showed great concern for Paula; she probably wasn't even aware that she hasn't been taking care of herself. Eating, sleeping…she needs her strength to handle these responsibilities.

The day arrived and the ceremony was beautiful. The turnout was larger than expected. After the ceremony, the funeral director handed Paula the urn. She was very shaky so Rebecca carried the urn for her. Immediately after, they drove to the Verde River. When they arrived, the girls agreed it is a beautiful area. Paula began to scatter the ashes as she spoke her final goodbye.

"Bill I've always loved you and I always will. You brought such happiness in my life and I will never forget you. We cannot be together in this life; but someday we will be together again and then it will be forever. Goodbye my love."

Rebecca couldn't help but cry; together they stood crying and comforting each other. Ten minutes later they were on their way home. Paula never spoke a word. Even though she needed to move on with her life it is just as important that she has time to grieve. The ride was long and quiet, kind of relaxing. When they arrived at the apartment, Paula sat on the balcony for a while. As much as Rebecca wanted to do something, she let her have time to herself, but she stayed there in case she was needed. Rebecca made some plans to present to Paula the next day

By tomorrow, she thought it would be a good idea to try and get her going again.

The night was restless for Paula; all she dreamed about was Bill. A perfectly natural thing after a losing someone you love. When morning arrived she was ready to move on, so she thought, until Rebecca told her what she had in mind.

"I think I'll go back to work tomorrow. It'll help me take my mind off things."

"Honey, you still need some time for yourself, it's much too early to go back to work."

"Ok. What do you suggest?"

"I was thinking a getaway for a week. Here are some brochures on a ranch lodge I was looking at. They have many activities and so much to do. Anything from horseback riding to hiking and party's spas and sightseeing. The rooms are beautiful and I think it will do us both good. You could really use this time Paula. What do you think?"

Skimming over the brochures, Paula thought a few moments. This could be a good idea, but it didn't seem right. However, she did need to move on and get her life back together again.

"Well, there is a monument there I've always wanted to see.

Maybe you're right, this could be a good idea."

"Great! I made the reservations and we were lucky. They had a cancellation so I grabbed it right away."

"You're pretty sure of yourself, what if I said no?"

"We've been friends for three years and I think that's long enough to know what I can and cannot assume. By the way, I packed your things so we can leave, I just need to swing by my place to pack."

"Are you sure this is right?"

"Well, look at you. You were ready to go back to work. You need some time, so why not at the lodge. We can stay in the room or get out and do something. I think a getaway is a good start, that way you can ease into moving ahead."

Before long, the girls were packed and on their way to the ranch lodge. They talked along the way, planning their week. The scenery was beautiful they couldn't believe they never planned a trip like this before. Rebecca couldn't help but notice a smile on Paula's face. This was going to be a great trip. They drove straight to the lodge without stopping, and before long, they arrived. Just ahead was the lodge; the girls were excited to start their week. People all around looking like they were having a great time. There was a group coming back from horseback riding.

"Here we are; I'll run in and get the key to our room, then we'll get settled. Be right back."

Paula waited in the car, just looking over the area. For a brief moment, she saw a man who looked exactly like Bill! Staring at him, she was ready to call out to him when Rebecca opened the car door.

"Let's go, I have the key. Paula. Are you alright?"

"Of course, I'm fine. Let's go get settled."

They retrieved their bags from the trunk of the car and went inside. Paula went straight out to the patio and sat down. Rebecca didn't say anything; she didn't want to push her too much. It was obvious what was on her mind, but by the end of their trip, she was convinced Rebecca she would be just fine.

"How would you feel about eating in tonight and getting started on our vacation tomorrow? We'll be here all week and the ride was a bit exhausting."

"That sounds fine. I am a bit tired myself."

Rebecca fixed dinner in the kitchenette while Paula unpacked. She even checked their cameras to make sure they were loaded and had fresh batteries. They had dinner on the patio then played some cards until dusk set. In the distance, you could hear the sounds of festivities, but even still, it was a peaceful night. A gentle breeze kissed their faces and the sky was packed with stars. The leaves on the trees seemed to wave and the air was so fresh. The girls were relaxed. They and finally grew tired enough to turn in for the night.

At the break of dawn, the girls were up and getting ready to begin their vacation. First on the list was the monument Paula wanted to see. Rebecca was excited about this vacation, and Paula seemed a bit excited herself, which made Rebecca happy. When they arrived at Montezuma's Castle, it was still early, hardly anyone was there this time in the morning. They started taking pictures before they even went on the tour.

"Rebecca, this is incredible! It's a five story, twenty room dwelling, and so well preserved!"

"It is very beautiful. It must take a lot of work to preserve this."

How great it was to see Paula so excited about something, especially after all she has been through. When the tour was over, the guide offered to take their picture in front of the monument. They thanked their guide, then took one last look before leaving. On their way back, they talked about horseback riding and hiking. Paula drove back this time so Rebecca could enjoy the scenery.

Back at the lodge they had checked for available horses. They were booked up the rest of the day so Paula booked a spot for the next day.

"How about we workout, then go to the spa? To tell you the truth, Rebecca, I do have some nervous nerves I could work off. The monument was great, but I have this nervous energy."

"I understand what you're saying. Actually, I could use a workout myself. After that, we'll do a sauna, then a hot tub, then rub downs and facials."

They relieved a lot of tension. While getting their rub down, Paula asked Rebecca about her boyfriend, Wes.

"I'm not trying to pry, but I noticed that Wes wasn't at the ceremony for Bill. I thought he liked Bill?"

"He did, but presently we're not talking. Let's not get into that right now and just concentrate on relaxing. That's why we came here."

"Is there anything I can do? You've been helping me with Bill's death, there must be something I can do for you."

"There is, have fun."

Paula felt terrible but let it go for now. Next, they had facials, manicure, and pedicures. When they were through, they felt like a million bucks. So, of course they decided to go to the casino and do a little gambling. Later, after dinner, there was a show, which rounded off the day perfectly, almost like being in Vegas. They played the slot machines, blackjack, and even craps. They didn't win very much, but it sure was fun trying. They had a couple of drinks before they went back to their room for the night. This time, Rebecca was a bit out of sorts. Paula thought she would try again to talk to her.

"Rebecca, I'm very sorry about bringing up Wes, but wouldn't you feel better if you talked about it? It helped me, remember?"

"I don't think so."

"I can see you're upset. Are you going to let whatever is bothering you spoil your trip? If you talk about, it you may be able to get past it, whatever it may be."

"I'm sorry you're right. The night that Bill was…well, anyway, we argued that night. Thinking back, it was silly. I do plan on calling him when we get back home but right now we're on vacation."

"You still didn't tell me much. Talk to me, what happened?"

"Well, he's been really busy at work, and I know that. still I was upset because he missed my birthday. I should know better, and he even offered to make it up to me. I was just being selfish. I accused him of going out with another woman. I acted like a spoiled brat. Anyway, when things happened to Bill, I never had a chance to call him. You needed me, my relationship can wait."

"I can't believe you would do that, even for me! You love him."

"I do, but now it will have to wait. You're more important right now, and if Wes and I were talking, he would agree. He thinks a lot about you."

"Another woman! Even I know how much Wes loves you. I cannot believe he would see another woman."

"I know that, I was just hormonal at the time. You understand, and so will he, when I call him after we get back home."

"Don't wait, call him now and settle this, you'll feel so much better."

"Maybe after the hike tomorrow, we'll see how I feel."

A good night's sleep is probably what she needed, although they were still not quit tired yet. They brought along a book to read just for times like this. Before very long, they were asleep. The next day they were up and ready for the hike. Their backpacks were ready to go. They dressed and went out the door. The horses were reserved for the afternoon so they had all morning if they wanted. They enjoyed the hike, even though they had sore muscles from the workout yesterday, but it was tolerable. They lost track of all time, they were enjoying themselves so much. The sky was clear and so blue, the air fresh as can be, and the conversation eased their minds of any problems either of them have. They sat for a while in the grass listening to the bird's chirp, trees and bushes all around, and the smell of pine from the pine trees. Paula looked at her watch. When they realized they were gone for two hours, they headed back to their room to clean up for lunch, after lunch they were riding horses. Paula was never on a horse but Rebecca was a few times. They rode horses the remainder of the afternoon. When they came back, Paula had a carrot put aside for her horse, so when no one was looking she fed it to him.

Paula never thought of Bill, even once, and their appetite weakened them, so they cleaned up and rushed to the steakhouse for dinner. When they entered, the aroma made their mouths water. Everyone was talking about the big party at the end of the week and Rebecca couldn't wait to attend. After dinner the girls went back to their room exhausted. It was a nice kind of tired. Not stressful, like when you come home from work, but relaxing. The moon was big and bright, and there were just enough stars to accent the sky. You can see both the big and little dippers, it was heaven. She and Paula relaxed so much in their beds, they drifted off to sleep.

That night Bill came back to Paula, her eyes opened slowly to see him standing there next to her bed, the moon was shining behind him. It was then he spoke to her.

"I'll always love you, Paula, but you need to let me go now. We'll be together again someday, but now you have to live and enjoy your life. Be happy in your life Paula, and remember I'll always love you. Good night, my love."

Slowly waking up, Paula sat up in bed and looked all around. Rebecca was still sleeping. She went to the window and looked up at the sky.

"I'll always love you, too, Bill."

She blew a kiss towards the sky as a tear ran down her cheek. This was Bill's last gift to her. Now she really can get on with her life. Paula wasn't scared, or even upset; it was comforting to her.

When morning arrived, Paula was up and was cooking Rebecca's favorite breakfast, blueberry pancakes, sausage, grapefruit, and coffee.

"Well, aren't you up early and cooking breakfast! What's going on?"

"I had the most beautiful dream last night. I'll tell you over breakfast. After all, this is our last day, and we want to make the most of it, don't we?"

"Yes, we do. It's really nice to see you in better spirits."

Paula wanted to cram a little bit of everything in before the party, and came close to doing it all. Rebecca was amazed at the change in her and her energy, but that was just fine. There was a dress shop nearby, so they decided to buy new dresses for the party. Something colorful. It was getting late, so they bought what they wanted and went back to their room to change.

"I can't wait. I walked by the club and the aroma from the food poured out of the room, it smells great!"

"Don't stop there, Paula, tell me more!"

"That's all I have. I was so anxious about the party, I wanted to get back here so we can get ready."

They both wore beautiful, brightly colored dresses, and a flower in their hair. In practically no time, they were on their way to the Fiesta Room. This will be the piece de resistance of their trip. They walked into the room and it was like walking across the border into Mexico. The men wore sombreros and the women were given chili pepper bracelets. The band was playing Latin Fiesta, the food, all Mexican, and the place settings at the tables had maraca's as party favors. There were even piñatas hanging from the ceiling. At the end of the food tables, there was a fountain of margarita's flowing. What a wonderful evening this would be, everyone so happy and carefree and just enjoying themselves.

The girls were asked to dance, and after dinner, Paula started a Conga line. The party was alive, and the room filled with laughter, happiness, and dancing. The music stopped once, long enough for the band to take a break. Everyone was having a great time. Rebecca wished this night could last forever, but at two in the morning, everything closed down. The girls went back to their room and collapsed.

"Rebecca, did you enjoy yourself as much as I did?"

"Yes I did, we are definitely going to have to come back here next year."

"Sounds like a plan to me."

They changed their clothes then sat in the lounge chairs on the patio for some fresh air, they fell asleep from exhaustion due to all the excitement of the Cinco De Mayo celebration.

The next morning the sun shined brightly, waking Paula. She woke Rebecca so they could have breakfast and pack up to go back home to reality. This week just seemed to fly by; they really had a great time at the lodge. Rebecca stopped at the store for a few things, then they were quickly back on the road again. Paula found some soft music on the radio then leaned back in her seat to soak up some sun.

"Paula, I thought we could stop at my place first. I'll fix us some lunch, then we can go to your apartment and I'll help you with anything you need done."

"Sounds fine."

The ride home didn't seem as long as it was when they went to the lodge. When they arrived, Rebecca parked the car, Paula helped with the luggage and groceries. They did some unpacking. Rebecca prepared lunch and Paula turned on the radio. She poured a couple of iced teas. That was the best trip they had taken in a very long time. There was a news bulletin on the radio.

"The police are still investigating the murder of a local man, Wes Adams. We have no new updates at this time. Police are asking for help with this case. Anyone with any information about this murder please call police…"

"Paula! Please tell me I heard that wrong! I could not have heard the name I thought I did."

"Rebecca, calm down. I'll call and see what I can find out."

Paula called and found out what she could. What she did find out wasn't pleasant. They needed someone to come in and identify his body. Since his family lives on the East coast, the only one who could go in would be Rebecca.

"Well I suppose I should go. What choice do I have? Paula, would you mind going with me?

"You don't even have to ask. Whenever you're ready, I'll take you."

Paula drove to the morgue. Rebecca was getting very nervous and not so sure she could go through with this. All she could think of was, please let there be a mistake.

"I just need a moment, I'll be fine. Really."

Rebecca was praying that this wouldn't be Wes. Until now, she really didn't have an idea how Paula felt when this happened to her. Why all the sudden madness, and why Wes and Bill? Please God; please don't let it be him. A couple deeper breaths and in she would go. Lieutenant

Garrett was there to escort her in, as well as Paula. This was not an easy thing for anyone to go through. Rebecca began to feel a bit faint; one more deep breath before she identified the body.

James pulled the handle and the drawer slid open. He only lifted the sheet enough to expose his face.

"Oh my God, it's Wes!"

"Calm down, I'm here for you."

"Someone took him from me, why?"

Rebecca turned and ran out the door. James Garrett was right behind her to assist her and get her to the ladies' room. Paula was there to help while she was in the stall getting sick. Paula stepped out a brief moment to speak with James.

"What's going on and why is this happening? Have you found any suspects yet?"

"I'm very sorry, we haven't. As to why this is happening, we can't make a connection between Bill and Wes to even give us a clue. The only connection we have with them, are you two women. Their jobs were different, they worked different hours. At this time, it appears these are random murders, but for what reason, we're still working on that."

"This is crazy! It makes no sense."

"Is there anything at all you can think of that could help us?"

"If there were, we would certainly tell you. I'm sorry, but I need to get back to Rebecca. Please find and stop this maniac."

"Miss Lived, just one more question. Is there anything you can tell me about Wes Adams that may help me?"

"I wish I could, but we just came back to town today. We've been gone all week. When we got in, she was preparing lunch and I turned on the radio. That was when we heard about Wes. Now if you don't mind, I have to get back to her."

Rebecca opened the door and told Paula she had to get out of there and wanted to go home. They turned and left as quickly as they could. The fresh air on the way home helped eased her nausea, some but it couldn't take the pain away. When they arrived back at her apartment, there was a message from Rebecca's boss, Mr. Duncan. He couldn't give her anymore paid time off, but he could give her a leave of absence. Paula called him and made arrangements with him for Rebecca. Paula also called her boss, there was a big shipment of merchandise coming in and he couldn't spare her any longer, but agreed to work with her anyway he could. Rebecca wasn't hungry, so Paula gave her a sleeping pill and told her she would be back as soon as she could.

This used to be a peaceful town, until some monster decided to terrorize it, and for what reason? Why would anyone want to kill anyone like Bill and Wes? With an ax yet! Some sick crazy monster is out there and until they are caught no one will rest easy. Paula left but before the pill would take effect, Rebecca called Wes's parents. This wasn't going to be easy. She never even met his parents and now she has to be the one to tell them their son is gone. The phone was ringing and a woman answered. She answered as Mrs.

Adams. After she told her about her son, she could hear her crying, wishing she could be there for her and comfort her.

"Mrs. Adams, I can't tell you how sorry I am. I'll be making arrangements to bring his body home to be buried as soon as possible. I'll call you when the plane lands. I wish we could get together under better circumstances."

"Rebecca, are you sure you want to do this? His father and I can come there to handle things."

"I'm sure. Besides, I would come there anyway. A round trip for me would be better because, of course, I would come there for the funeral anyway. You have enough to do on your end; I'll bring him home to you. According to the airlines I'll arrive about ten fifteen in the morning. I'll see you then."

"My Wes has written many letters and spoke of you often. You meant a great deal to him. Now that I have a chance to talk to you, I can tell you're every bit as wonderful as he described. I can't thank you enough."

The sleeping pill was kicking in; Rebecca ended the call and went to the bedroom to rest. She cried for a while then finally went to sleep. At the store, Mr. Langdon and Paula were discussing what has happened in the past couple of weeks as they worked on the stores shipment.

"Paula, please understand, I feel just terrible about what's happened with you and your friend. I'd like to be able to do more, but I do have a business to run. I'm not trying to be cold hearted…"

"Oh, I don't think that at all, and neither does she. We do understand, it's these crazed acts upon Bill and Wes we don't understand."

"It makes no sense at all. Such a waste of two innocent men. If it's any consolation, I'm sure the police will find whoever did this."

"I'm sure they will, but before, or after they kill again? I'm sorry, really I am. This is just so frustrating. Rebecca is taking Wes home to be buried and I told her I would take her to the airport. Would you mind if I were a little late tomorrow? The rest of what I am doing to help her with can be done after work."

"That's fine. In fact, we are slow today and we're almost done with the shipment. Why don't you go ahead and take the rest of the day when we're through and I'll see you when you get here tomorrow."

"Thank you so much, Mr. Langdon I do appreciate this."

When Paula was through, she left and picked up some take out for dinner. She drove straight over to Rebecca's. She was still resting, and as much as she hated to wake her, she had to eat.

"Wake up, I brought some take out so we can have dinner and talk."

Paula was serving when Rebecca came in, placing a small black velvet box on the table.

"What is this?"

"Go ahead, open it. I found this in his nightstand."

Inside was a beautiful diamond engagement ring. Obviously, Wes was going to propose to Rebecca.

"I'm thinking I should return it, what do you think?"

"Wes was going to ask you to marry him with this ring. I think it's something you should keep; it would be his last gift to you. If you don't, you may regret it later. What if he already proposed and you had it before this ludicrously? It would be yours anyway! I think he would want you to have this."

"Maybe you're right, I don't know. I don't know anything anymore."

She thought for a moment. Maybe Paula was right and maybe she would keep the ring. Whatever, it would have to wait until she came home. There was packing and details she had to take care of before the flight in the morning.

"You know, three weeks ago we were all living our lives in our same every day fashion. Now, because of some maniac, our lives are turned upside-down. It makes no sense, none at all."

"No, it doesn't, but I'm sure the police will find him and bring him to justice."

"What is justice for killing innocent people? Whatever they do, it won't bring Bill and Wes back again.

Paula held her tight to comfort her; only what's happened is not a comfort. They would both need time to deal with this. She helped Rebecca to pack and spent the night, in case she would need anything, or someone to talk to about her feelings.

"Hopefully the police will have this all solved by the time you get back. It won't bring back Bill and Wes, but there will be closure. Try to get some rest, you have a plane to catch in the morning."

"I'm not so sure I can do this, but I promised his mother. What am I going to do?"

"Listen to me. I know you, you're a strong person. You can pull through anything, I've seen you. Now, I know a family who is planning the burial of their son and I know you want to do this for them."

"I never even met them, what was I thinking?"

"You were thinking of taking care of Wes one last time and helping his family pull through this. Think of it this way, how are you going to feel if you don't do this?"

"I'll regret it the rest of my life."

"Alright then, there is your answer. I know how much you loved him, and because of that love, you can't not do this."

"You're right, I can't not do this. I want to do this."

"I can't get any more time off or I would go with you."

"Don't worry, I'll be fine. I was someday looking forward to meeting his parents, but not like this." Early the next day the girls were at the airport and said their goodbyes. Paula stayed until the plane was off the ground, then went to work. The day was steady. A usual day in the store. There were even some tourists stopping in for souvenirs. After work, Paula finished off Wes's apartment. When she arrived home, there was a message from Rebecca letting her know she arrived safely, and thanking her for all her help. A long soak in a hot bubble bath sounded perfect, maybe even a glass of wine. Lots of lit candles and some soft music made this evening perfect. If only it could be perfect for Rebecca.

CHAPTER 2

Two days later, Paula was finishing her work when Mr. Langdon approached her.

"I want to commend you. After all you and your friend have been through, you still manage to do a fine job here at the shop. I realize how difficult this must be on both of you, so doing your job cannot be easy, yet you struggle to do the best you can."

"Well, yes and no. When I'm working, my mind is occupied so I don't have the time to think. It's when I'm not working that makes it so hard to get through the day without uncomfortable thoughts."

"I understand, which is why I was thinking about taking you out to dinner this evening. I have nothing planned, and we both have to eat dinner. I was hoping a night out would help relieve the stress of everything and we can keep each other company. Alone, you stand a better chance of reliving all this. What do you say?"

Paula thought about it a moment and knew what he said was the truth. Besides, she really didn't feel like being alone tonight anyway.

"I'd love to, I probably won't hear from Rebecca, being as busy as she is with his family. Thank you so much I really appreciate the offer."

"I'll be finished in ten minutes then we can leave."

After Mr. Langdon finished what he needed to do, they left the shop locking the door behind them. They talked over dinner. He was telling Paula about his plans to expand his shop. His place was small but very successful. It was about time to expand and bring in new merchandise. Paula had some suggestions and Mr. Langdon liked what he heard. He jotted everything down in his notebook and Paula was more than glad to assist anyway she could.

"Well, dinner was great and so was the company. If you like, I can follow you home to make sure you're safe?"

"That's sweet, but no thank you. I'll be fine, really. Thank you for dinner."

He at least walked her to her car and waited for her to drive away before he left. She drove home, poured herself some iced tea, then collapsed on her sofa. There was a movie on television she wanted to watch: tuned in and watched TV until she was sleeping. The day was long and she was exhausted. It was midmorning when she woke up the next day. There was a news bulletin on that another man was murdered.

"My God, what is happening in this town?"

The phone rang. It was Rebecca calling to check in with Paula. They talked briefly; she wanted to get back to the family. Paula didn't mention the murder that had happened last night. She would find out soon enough when she came home, besides, she had enough on her mind right now. Everything was as well as could be expected and Rebecca told her she should be home in a couple of days. Then they can catch up on events.

"Take care, Rebecca, I'll see you when you get back. Please extend my sympathies to the Adams. I'll see you soon."

There was a knock at the door and Paula went to see who it was. What a surprise to see James standing there.

"Hello, Miss Lived."

"Lieutenant Garrett! How can I help you?"

"Are you aware of a murder that took place last night? A Mr. Mark Johnston."

"Yes, I am, I just heard about it on the news a few minutes ago. What does this have to do with me?"

"Did you know him?" "No, I didn't. Just what are you implying?"

"Nothing at all, I'm sorry. It's just the only connection we had with the other two murders are you and your friend. I was just wondering if maybe you would have happened to know this one. Believe me I'm not suggesting anything; we're just looking for a common denominator. A connection, a motive, something to go on."

"I didn't know him and Rebecca is out of town. She took Wes back home. Are you saying you don't even know why this is happening?"

"We don't know. We don't know why these murders happened. Again, I'm very sorry. I'm not trying to implicate you; just searching for a pattern, or something, that will help us find this lunatic. I'm sorry to have bothered you, and please accept my apologies. Have a nice day."

"We'll all have a nice day when this is over, Lieutenant."

She slammed the door and sat down on the sofa, wondering when there would be an end to this madness. She noticed a bag on the chair, across the room. She went over to pick up the bag and looked through it. Inside were the pictures she and Rebecca had taken on their trip. A great week that ended in tragedy. Paula went into the kitchen to make some coffee and go through the pictures. She found a picture she didn't know was taken. Rebecca must have sneaked that one; it was Paula at the head of the conga line. She thought out loud to herself:

"Rebecca, we will be able to get our lives back, once the police find the killer. It won't be the same without Bill and Wes, but we'll manage."

Rebecca, was helping Mrs. Adams with the food for family and friends, many still in tears over the loss of Wes. His mother had an enlarged picture of him in the living room for everyone to remember him. When Rebecca walked into the kitchen, Mrs. Adams was having a moment to herself.

"Mrs. Adams."

"Please, call me Louise. You know Wes was very much in love with you. He always wrote or called and was sure to mention you every time. He talked a lot about spending the rest of his life with you."

Again she broke down and Rebecca did what she could to try to comfort her. She held her close, doing her best to help her through this.

"You know, Wes is someone anyone can be proud of, he was a hard worker. He cared about his family and everyone loved him."

"Your right, he is someone we can all be proud of. I just don't understand how anyone can do such an awful thing to another human being. I should have been the one to go first, I was prepared for that. He was my baby and had his whole life ahead of him."

One look at Rebecca and she realized that she too was missing him every bit as much as anyone in the family.

"I'm so sorry, I know you're feeling a loss like the rest of us. I don't mean to ignore your feelings. I do appreciate all you've done, bringing him back here to be buried. You're every bit as special as he described you. We better get back in there."

"Before we do, remember, he will always be with us and no one can take that away from us."

"You're right, thank you. Now, we better get in there before we're missed."

There was a large crowd of people attending. It was clear just how much people loved Wes. Rebecca could feel both, the love, and the pain everyone was feeling. Hours later everyone was leaving and Rebecca helped to clean up. She tried doing most of it whenever Mrs. Adams wasn't looking.

"Well, you'll be leaving tomorrow. You know you're welcome to stay another day or two, if you'd like. We love having you here."

"Thank you I wish I could stay longer, but I have to get back to my job."

"I can't thank you enough for all you've done. I just want you to know you're welcome here anytime. We do hope to see you again. Wes told us he was going to propose to you. He loved you very much. The day he told me that, I went out and bought a little something for you. There may not be a marriage, but I would still like you to have this."

She opened the package and was surprised to find a pearl necklace and earrings.

"Louise, they're beautiful! I'm not so sure I should take them. It just doesn't seem right."

"Wes wrote many letters telling us all about you. After so many letters and phone calls, it's as though you're already family. These past few days you participated in this funeral, just as any family member would. Please, I'd really like for you to have them."

"Thank you so much. This is really sweet of you."

"If there's anything you ever need, or even just need to talk, call us anytime. You are family."

"I promise; I will keep in touch. Thank you again. Well, I'd better turn in; I have a flight to catch tomorrow. Good night."

The next morning, they ate breakfast, then drove her to the airport. They were sorry to see her go and had hoped she would return again. Goodbyes were said before Rebecca boarded the plane. The flight back was smooth and quiet. She couldn't wait to get back home and see Paula. She has so much to tell her. His family was terrific! She actually felt like a member of his family. It didn't seem long before the plane landed. As soon as she was off, there was Paula standing there, waiting for her. Rebecca seemed a little solemn. She rushed over hugging her. They were so happy to see each other.

"It's so good to see you. I want to hear everything about your trip. How did it go? Don't leave out a single detail."

"The flight was great and so were his family. That's how they treated me, like I was a member of their family. They were really wonderful."

"Let's drop off your luggage and I'll take you to lunch. Are you hungry?"

"Not very."

They went to her apartment and unpacked some things. Rebecca pulled out the box Louise gave her before she left.

"What's in the box?"

"Wes told his mother he was going to marry me. She was going to give these to me to wear at the wedding and wanted me to have them even though…even though there will be no wedding."

She handed the box to Paula. Opening the box, she saw how lovely the pearls looked, at the very least expensive.

"They're beautiful. She must think a lot of you to want you to have them."

"I know. I can't wear these, or the ring, at least not now. I'll just tuck them away for safe keeping, until the time comes when I feel I can wear them. Let's get some lunch."

They went to a café nearby and decided to have their lunch outside. They sat at a table near a tree. Then placed their orders with the waitress. James Garrett was leaving the café when he saw the girls seated and approached them.

"Miss Travis, I'm sorry to bother you, but I've already spoken to Miss Lived. At that time, you were out of town… did you have a nice trip back?"

"I can't say it was pleasant, under the circumstances, but it went well. Paula filled me in on your visit to her so if you're going to ask me if I knew the last victim, I didn't. Mr. Johnston, I believe."

"It was, and thank you. I hate to put you through this, especially after all you both have been through, but I am just doing my job. I'm sorry to disturb you. Enjoy your lunch, on me. Have a nice day."

He left after dropping a twenty-dollar bill on the table.

"Can you believe him? He has to be joking, thinking we would have anything to do with these murders."

"He may begin thinking differently now, since neither of us know Mr. Johnston, or that you were out of town. I was angry at first myself, then I realized, he is just doing his job."

They looked at each other and smiled.

"Hey, take a look at these pictures! I had them developed while you were away. They turned out pretty nice."

Pausing for a moment, Rebecca looked at Paula.

"Are you scared? I mean, nothing like this has ever happened in our town before, why now? People are living in fear, it's not right."

"I know, but the police will catch him, I'm sure. Garrett made it clear they won't stop until he's found."

Rebecca had an enigmatic look on face, then looked through the pictures. She wasn't as sure about things as Paula, but she would forget about it for now. After lunch, they stopped at the bank where Rebecca worked, to talk to her boss about coming back to work. They did a little window shopping, then decided to take in a movie. A comedy may lift their spirits. They bought some popcorn and soft drinks, then went in and found a seat. The movie was great and it took their minds off things, if only for a while. When it was over, they went outside and talked about it a while. They saw a strange man staring at them.

Casually, they walked towards the car, he seemed to be following them. They sat in the car and locked the doors while Paula called the police on her cell phone. Scared, they patiently waited for the police. There were still plenty of people in the lot. Minutes later, a car parked close to Rebecca and Paula. The man in it looked like James Garrett. Paula's phone rang. It was Garrett. Without turning, or pointing with her fingers, she told him where the man was. Garrett stepped out of his car, walked towards him, grabbed his arm, and cuffed him.

"Let's make this easy! Answer my questions and no one has to know what's going on, understand?"

"What have I done? I'm just standing here."

"Why are you following those girls?"

"I was admiring one of them. Is it a crime to be interested in a woman?"

"I don't recall ever seeing you around here, where are you from?"

"I'm here on vacation, visiting my sister and brother-in-law."

"What are their names?"

"Alex and Cassidy Hirsch."

He also gave him their address and phone number.

"Am I under arrest! What's going on?"

Garrett had one of the backup officers call in and run a check. The report came back and cleared his story.

"Alright, you're not from around here, but are you aware of the murders that have taken place in the past three weeks?"

"I have heard about them but I didn't kill anyone."

"Your name is Shawn Hastings?"

"That's right."

"These two ladies had fiancé's and they both were victims in these murders. Of course, they're going to be scared. Watch how you handle things in the future and enjoy the rest of your stay. Sorry for the inconvenience."

"I'm very sorry, I didn't mean to scare them. Would you express my apologies to them?"

"I will, now you go on home and stay out of trouble."

He walked over their car to let them know they were safe.

"I'm sorry ladies, he asked me to extend his apologies. He didn't mean to scare you; he was admiring the two of you. Probably trying to work up the courage to ask you out is all that was. He's here visiting his sister on vacation and should be leaving soon. You did the right thing, calling us. Would you like one of us to follow you home?"

"Thanks, but we'll be fine. Goodnight."

Rebecca dropped off Paula at her apartment.

"Call me the minute you get home! I want to make sure you're alright."

"I will, I'll wait here until you're in the door. Sweet dreams."

Once Paula was inside, she drove home and called her immediately after she was inside her apartment. She walked over to her dresser and pulled out the pearls and the ring. How could she wear these, it wasn't right? Tears came to her eyes; she cried a while, then locked them in a lock box, storing them in her closet. Maybe, just maybe, someday she would be able to wear them.

After work the next day, Brad Duncan, president of the bank, called Rebecca into his office.

"Please have a seat. Tomorrow is my wife's birthday and I'm planning a cookout and some friends over. I know this is short notice, but you were away when I made the plans. If you don't feel up to it, I'll understand, but I invited everyone from the bank. You're welcome to bring a friend with you, and it sure would be nice to see you there. We have a pool, so I told everyone to bring their swimsuits. "

She was thinking. Mr. Duncan could tell she may have some doubts.

"We're all very sorry about what happened to Wes, please don't think we're being disrespectful. I just think it would be nice for you to be around some friends. You and a friend can go swimming and enjoy yourselves, hopefully. Take your mind off things. What do you say?"

"Sounds like fun. I'm sure my friend would love to come. Thank you, Mr. Duncan."

"Great! Don't forget your swimsuits. We're here for you, too, if there's anything you need. Please don't hesitate to ask."

On the way home, she stopped to pick up Paula and told her about the party her boss was having. The invitation was extended to her as well.

"I think it's a great idea. It won't be easy, but we need to move on with our lives. They would want us to, you know that, don't you?"

"I know, but it doesn't make it any easier. It will take our minds off things."

They stopped at the state store to pick up some wine for dinner and a special bottle for Mr. Duncan. While Paula was picking out the wine, Rebecca was in the grocery store picking up something for dinner. They unloaded the car when they arrived home.

"I bought your favorite for dessert, chocolate mocha cake."

"You're a doll, thank you so much. I'm going to start dinner and I bought special wrapping for the wine. I'll wrap the wine, then set the table."

They talked over dinner. Rebecca went into a little more detail about her trip back East and Paula talked about her boss, Mr. Langdon, wanting to expand his shop. They even talked more about the party the next day. Paula talked Rebecca into spending the night. Neither of them really wanted to be alone. They had cake and coffee and played some cards. It was difficult taking their minds off things, but they did their best.

Saturday afternoon arrived. The girls were on their way to Mr. Ducan's home while Rebecca talked about the party. This was something he did every year for his wife, and he always invited everyone at the bank. They would cook on the grill, swim and dance. He went to such lengths for her. It was as though they were celebrating Christmas. Lanterns were strung all around, a table covered with rose petals held fruits and desserts. One section of the yard had a pond with a water fountain surrounded with white lights. It was clear to a blind man how much in love with his wife he was, to go to such lengths. Rebecca told Paula she would have a great time; they did every year. When they arrived, Mr. Duncan answered the door and invited them in, showing them to the yard where everything was set up. It was just as Rebecca described it. So very beautiful.

"Thank you Mr. Duncan for inviting me, Rebecca described what this would be like but it's even more beautiful to see it all."

"Thank you, Paula. I hope the two of you will enjoy yourselves. Both of you deserve to have a great time. We all work so hard, we need the playtime to relax and unwind. Help yourselves. There is a bartender and some appetizers. I'll be grilling shortly. Hope you brought your suits, the water is great. Enjoy."

"Paula, wait until you see the cake. He usually keeps it in the basement until he's ready. His daughter and son roll it out and there are balloons fastened to the cart. He really goes all out."

People were mingling. The yard was full and the music was festive. This was more like a very casual wedding than a birthday party. His wife was a very lucky woman. A very attractive man had approached Paula. Dark, and leaning towards the muscular side. It was clear he was interested in Paula, but she just wasn't ready for that yet.

"Hello, my name is Bruce. I couldn't help noticing you from across the yard. I don't remember seeing you here last year."

"Hi! I wasn't; I'm here with my friend, Rebecca. My name is Paula."

"I'm Uncle Brad's nephew. I'm moving here from out of town. If it's all right with you, I'd really like to get to know you better. Could we get together some time?"

"I'm sorry Bruce, but I really can't. I recently lost my fiancé. He was killed and I'm really not ready to go out with anyone yet. I hope you understand."

"I'm very sorry, of course I understand. Maybe sometime in the future when you are ready. I'll be around. It was very nice meeting you."

Rebecca showed Paula around and introduced her to Mr. Duncan's son and daughter, Kent and Jill. Everyone was so nice to Paula. All of them had a way of making you feel right at home. Everybody was having a great time when Kent came out asking everyone to hold it down. His father was bringing out his mother to surprise her. They needed complete silence. Seconds later, they stepped out on the patio. Everyone yelled surprise.

"Oh Brad, this is beautiful. You never fail to surprise me every year and I'm never the wiser. You would think I'd learn by now."

"I have my ways. Now, before we go on, you have to open your present. Happy birthday, Diane."

He gave her a box beautifully wrapped in gold. When she opened it, there was a beautiful diamond and emerald necklace. He helped her put it on. The lights reflection seemed to dance across her neck. When he kissed, her everyone applauded. The next thirty minutes were spent opening presents from all her friends; they were very generous.

"Thank you all so much, and for being here to share my special day with me. We enjoy having all of you here. That's my speech, so let's party!"

The music played and the guests danced and laughed, just enjoying themselves. Diane went around to thank each and every one personally for the gifts they brought. Later, everyone ate dinner, then the cake was brought out. A beautiful, two-tier cake with roses covering the top tier, Diane's favorite. They sang happy birthday before she cut the cake. Afterwards, guests were swimming and dancing. What a party! everyone was having a great time. The food was great and the evening so perfect for this party. It was almost nine thirty when the crowd was thinning out. What a gala time for everyone. Rebecca and Paula wished Diane a happy birthday before leaving and thanked them for the invitation. Diane and Brad walked them both to the door and said goodnight.

"Thank you both for coming. Drive carefully."

Paula noticed something was wrong with Rebecca as they were leaving.

"Are you alright?"

"I'm fine I just had too much…."

She fell to the ground and Paula called for help. Both Brad and Diane ran out the door to see what had happened when they saw Rebecca on the ground.

"What happened?"

"I don't know. She was walking slowly so I asked her what was wrong. She was trying to say something when she fainted."

"Brad, her pulse is rapid, we need to get her to the hospital now."

"I can take her but I need help getting her to the car."

Brad picked her up and carried her to the car. Diane gave Paula their number to call them.

"Please call us as soon as you know what's wrong or if you need anything. I mean that."

"I know you do, and I will. Thank you."

Diane and Brad stood and watched as Paula sped out of the driveway.

She rushed as quickly as she could to get her to the emergency room. When she arrived, a nurse was there with a wheelchair after wheeling out a patient. Paula was able to get the nurse to help get Rebecca in the chair. The nurse told her to go check her in and she would take Rebecca to the back for treatment. Paula spoke to the receptionist and checked her in; all that was left is to wait. Worried about Rebecca, she paced back and forth in the waiting room. Almost an hour later, the nurse came out to talk to Paula.

"The doctor had some tests done and we're waiting for the results right now. It will be awhile longer. You can come back to see her, but just a few minutes, she needs to rest."

The nurse showed her to Rebecca's room and Paula stayed just a few minutes. She told her she would be in the waiting room when they released her, drinking cup after cup of coffee. Rebecca told her she was feeling fine now, but they needed to be sure before they could release her. The minutes were ticking away, but it seemed more like hours. Paula couldn't stop worrying about her. All she could think was what was taking them so long to find out what's going on with her. Maybe they weren't telling her everything; maybe there was something seriously wrong with Rebecca. A couple of hours later, Rebecca came out.

"Are you alright? Should you be walking? What happened?"

"I'm fine really, just too much to drink. Let's go to my place and we can talk over a cup of tea."

Paula wasn't convinced but didn't press her; she's been through enough for one evening. When they arrived at Rebecca's and were inside, she sat Paula down in the living room.

"I wanted to wait until we were here to tell you this."

"My God, something is wrong, isn't it? What is it, what's wrong?"

"Relax. Nothing is wrong, honest. Are you ready for this! I'm pregnant."

"You...you...you're pregnant! Is this for real or some kind of joke?"

"It's no joke, I'm pregnant. A part of Wes is growing inside me. I only wish he were here to enjoy this time with me. We had talked about having children. I'm hoping for a boy who looks just like Wes."

"They are sure that's what it is? You're not trying to keep anything from me, are you?"

"No, I'm not. I am pregnant!"

Paula jumped up throwing her arms around her. It's wonderful how something this beautiful can emerge from all the craziness that's been happening.

"This is great! I'm so happy for you! Will you be able to manage?"

"I will make it happen and I will manage. There is a part of Wes inside me and I'm not giving it up. Wes was taken from me, and now I'm blessed with his child. I'll do whatever it takes, I won't lose his child, too, nor will I give this baby up."

"No one is asking you to give up the baby. Of course, you can rely on me, but what I meant was your job."

"I have plenty of time to work on that, and I will. I want this baby and there isn't an obstacle that can, or will, force me to give up this child. I will have to manage. I need a few moments to myself. I'm going in my room and I'll be back in a bit."

"Alright, but I'm here if you need me. Did you even suspect pregnancy?"

"No, I didn't. I think this is fate because we were always so careful. I was meant to have this baby."

Rebecca went to her bedroom. Sitting on the edge of her bed, she picked up a picture of Wes from her nightstand and began talking to him.

"Oh Wes, I wish you could be here to share this miracle with me. Our baby is going to be so beautiful, I know that. I want a boy who looks just like you. Boy or girl, our baby will know everything there is to know about you. I promise you that. You've given me many wonderful gifts, but this gift is the best of all of them. Thank you. I'll always love you and our baby."

She placed the picture back on the stand then cried for a few moments. Rebecca was scared and happy, but no matter what, she was determined. After a short while, she joined Paula in the kitchen for some tea. Neither of them could sleep. The excitement of the baby kept them up talking the rest of the night. They talked so much that when they looked out the window, they found it was morning. Paula looked at the clock; it was after eight.

"Oh, I forgot, I was supposed to call your boss when we found out what was wrong. Let me call him now, then you should make a phone call his parents."

"They just buried their son, I don't know how they'll take this."

"They loved you, they'll love this. A part of their son will go on living. Why wouldn't that make them happy?"

"I hope you're right."

Paula called Diane and Rebecca called Louise. Everyone was thrilled about the news but was concerned as to how she would manage on her own. Mrs. Adams was in tears and couldn't have been happier. She was determined to raise this baby anyway she could. It is Sunday and Paula stayed so Rebecca could rest. She even planned a fancy dinner to celebrate the baby. Paula was on her way to the store. As she opened the door, there was Lieutenant Garrett ready to knock.

"Lieutenant, what a surprise, how can I help you?"

"I'm here to see Miss Travis. Is she in?"

"Hello, Mr. Garrett. You want to see me?"

"Yes. I have some information and I would like to ask you a few questions. We questioned a co-worker of Mr. Adams and he told us you and he had an argument. I believe it was before you went on your trip. Can you tell me what the argument was about?"

"It was a dumb argument. He broke a date with me, is all. Why is that so important?"

One look on his face and her question was answered.

"My God, you think I killed him, don't you? How could you think such a thing especially after I told you how much he meant to me? I personally flew his body back east for him to be buried near his family and you suspect me? Would a killer do such a thing?"

"Rebecca, please calm down!"

"Look, Lieutenant, you can't come in here upsetting her like this. She just found out she's pregnant. This kind of excitement is not good for her. They were very much in love and anyone who knew them, knew that about them. What does she have to gain by killing him?"

"I was hoping you could tell me."

"Really! How well did you check into things?"

"Rebecca!"

"No, he wants a motive and he thinks I have one. So, did you find an insurance policy? A will? Tell me what my motive is?"

"There was no insurance policy, or a will. However, it has been known of women killing for cheating. Maybe the argument was over another woman."

"Look, Rebecca and Wes loved each other deeply. Anyone would tell you that. Couples argue about broken dates, all the time that is not an out of the world thing. I suppose you think she killed Bill, too. Was that jealousy?"

"I'm sorry, I didn't mean to upset anyone. I'm just doing my job."

"If you really want to do your job, find the real killer. Goodbye!"

James left, closing the door behind him. Rebecca stood there looking like she was ready to burst into tears.

"Can you believe he thinks I killed Wes?"

"You're pregnant now you have to think of your baby. God forbid anything should happen, you can never get pregnant by Wes again. The police will do more investigating, and when they do, he'll realize what a mistake he made. In the meantime, you take care of you and that miracle inside of you. Things will work out, you'll see."

Before Paula left, she saw to it that Rebecca was resting until she came back from the store. She sat in her rocking chair in the bedroom, near the window, holding a box containing some letters and pictures. Underneath it all was book of poems Wes gave her on their first date. Wes must have asked her out a dozen times before she finally said yes. Every time he came in the bank, he would ask her out, and each time he gave her a single red rose hoping it would soften her. When she finally agreed to go out with him, he checked with other girls in the bank to see what her likes and dislikes were.

Wes planned a wonderful day with her, starting with a picnic lunch in the park. That was when he gave her the book of poems. They tossed a Frisbee, went for a walk, then later went to the lake. He had a rowboat waiting there for them, with some food to feed the ducks. Afterwards he drove her home to change for an evening of dinner and dancing. The night was just right and the moon couldn't have been bigger or brighter. You could almost reach out and touch it. He kissed her in the moonlight, holding her as close as he could. He was very impressionable that day.

A yellow envelope contained pictures of them on a trip to Utah. At Lake Powell, they went house boating, water-skiing, and even hiking to Rainbow Bridge. They had a wonderful time there. There are so many wonderful memories they shared, but now Wes is, himself, a memory. Someday she would share all these memories with their baby. Rebecca began thinking how lucky she really is. Paula lost her fiancé' and she is not pregnant. She does have material things to remember him by, but this is different. Rebecca has a part of Wes growing inside her, a child to raise and remind her everyday of her love for Wes. As difficult as it is burying the man in your life one week, then finding out your pregnant with his baby the next, she is lucky enough to still have a part of him growing inside her. Paula walked in the door with groceries. After setting them on the counter, she went in the bedroom to check on Rebecca. She is much calmer and looked so peaceful going through her box of treasures. Paula let her know she was back and offered to get her more tea before she started on dinner. A few minutes later, Paula came back without the tea. She wanted to let Rebecca know company was in the living room. When she went into the other room, she found Brad and Diane Duncan had stopped in to check on her.

"Brad and I wanted to see how you're doing, and bring you a gift for the baby and roses for you. Congratulations! We're very happy for you."

"Thank you, but it really wasn't necessary."

"Nonsense, all mothers to be and babies get fussed over. You're no exception. We also wanted to let you know we are here for you if you ever need anything, anything at all."

"She's right. If you ever need some time off, you know you can come to me and I'll be happy to make the arrangements. Rebecca you're like a member of our family, not just at the bank, but my family. Diane has always liked you, as well as my kids. We're serious, if you need anything, just let us know."

She thanked them for stopping by and promised she would come to them if there were anything she needed. She offered to help Paula in the kitchen, but she wouldn't hear of it. Instead, she handed Rebecca the mail to sort out and told her to go in the other room to relax. Today she planned on spoiling Rebecca all day. While looking through the mail, she came across a letter from an old school friend, Carolyn Brown. She hasn't heard from Carolyn since she moved away. Seems that Carolyn is pregnant, again. This will be her third baby! This time she named the baby Rebecca, after Rebecca Travis, because a long time ago she saved Carolyn's life.

Back in school, the two of them went shopping together often. On one of their shopping sprees, Carolyn was crossing the street as a car was heading her way. The brakes were gone and the driver couldn't stop. So Rebecca yanked her off the street. She promised her if she ever had a daughter she would name her Rebecca. She said she would, but Rebecca never took it to heart. She just figured it was one of those things you say when you're grateful for something, like saving your life. Apparently, Carolyn was serious. Enclosed was a picture of the baby. She was adorable. Rebecca had forgotten all about that incident back then but was very excited.

Immediately, she pulled out her stationary to write back, to thank her, and fill her in on what's been happening in her life. If only she didn't have anything bad to write about, but the pregnancy was a great thing she would save for last. She even suggested maybe someday they could get together. They weren't that far apart that either of them couldn't hop a Grey Hound bus for a visit. How wonderful it would be to see each other again. Once again, there was a knock at the door.

"May I help you?"

"Are you Rebecca Travis?"

"Yes I am; how may I help you?"

He handed her a large bouquet of beautiful flowers.

"Have a nice day."

They were beautiful and very fragrant. She was shocked when she opened the card that came with them. They were from Officer Garrett. He had felt terrible about upsetting her like he did and wanted to apologize. The perfume from the flowers filled the room, even Paula walked in to see what smelled so good.

"Wow, who are they from?"

"Take a look at the card."

"You know what? I'll bet this means you're no longer a suspect. Either that, or someone is smitten. Let me put them in water for you. They'll make a lovely center piece for the table."

Returning to her letter, she had one more item to add. By the third page the aroma from the kitchen broke Rebecca's concentration. She began feeling hungry and was going to ask Paula if she could use some help. She knew what her answer would be. In many ways, Rebecca considered herself lucky. For starters, she was wealthy with friends. That's what she had to think of, any time she felt lonely thinking about Wes. It may be awhile before that void in her heart would be filled. This is a different kind of lonely. The kind where you can be in a room filled with people, but still feel alone, the kind that only that special someone can fill. Someday, it would either get easier, or pass all together.

Paula called her for dinner, and what a dinner! Cherry glazed Cornish hens, wild rice, asparagus with hollandaise sauce and Caesar salad. For dessert, lemon sorbet Rebecca's favorite.

"Paula, you went to such trouble! You really shouldn't have!"

"I don't want to hear it, and it was no trouble. Remember, we're celebrating baby Travis."

They sat at the table enjoying their dinner; she even lit candles for a peaceful atmosphere. They talked about plans for the baby and Rebecca told her about the letter she received, showing Paula the picture Carolyn sent to her. Plans for the baby room were discussed. Rebecca saved the best for last, she asked Paula to be the godmother. Paula was so excited, of course she accepted. Then she began to make plans, but Rebecca told her she had plenty of time.

"There's no time like the present."

Rebecca couldn't help but laugh at Paula's excitement over the baby.

CHAPTER 3

The day was long and exhausting. Brad and Diane were getting ready to settle in when the clock struck eleven.

"Dian, are you coming to bed?"

"Not just yet, I'm still pretty alert. I'm going to finish this chapter, then I'll be in. You go on ahead, dear, I won't be too long."

Brad nestled in for the night while Diane finished. Once she picks up a book she's really interested in, it's difficult for her to put it down. She was always swept away by these romance novels. Twenty minutes later, she finished. She turned out the lights and did a quick door check, making sure they were locked. Starting up the stairs, knowing Brad would be asleep, she tip-toed to their bedroom. She quietly opened the door then let out a scream. Someone dressed in black, with a ski mask was ready to drop an ax on Brad, until Diane came into the room. Out the window flew the ax and the murderer tried to get out, but Brad latched on to his shirt. The murderer turned around and belted him across the face hard enough for him to land on the floor, while he made his escape. Diane ran over to check on Brad then looked out the window to see where he went. He was already gone and the ladder was laying on the ground. Quickly she picked up the phone to call the police. Brad joined Diane's side on the edge of the bed until she was off the phone.

"Brad you're bleeding! Let's get that taken care of. Whoever he was, he hit you pretty hard."

"Whoever he was, I can tell by the feel of his fist, it wasn't his bare fist. He had to have been using brass knuckles."

They went downstairs so she could make some coffee and get an ice pack for Brad. The doorbell rang and Brad went to let the police in. As he did, Diane walked in with a tray of coffee. She set the tray on the coffee table as they sat down to get a statement from the couple. Diane was still shaky, but did her best to cooperate. It had just occurred to her as they were talking, if she hadn't walked in when she did, she would be a widow right now. Her hands covered her face as she began crying.

"I don't understand why anyone would want to harm my husband? We never received any threats, and he never hurt anyone."

"Mrs. Duncan, there are no particular reasons for someone to commit such a crime. There are some who believe what they are doing is justifiable. A person can walk up to you on the street, decide they do not like the way you look or dress, so they pull a gun and shoot you. Some have a boyfriend or girlfriend, or even someone who had harmed them in some way and if they see someone who reminds them of that person, that is their reason to commit such an act. There is no rhyme or reason and makes no sense to anyone but themselves. That's all they need."

"Not only is that demented, but frightening. There has never been anything like that in this town before, so why now?"

"Diane, it's over. Don't upset yourself over this. Officer, is there a chance he may come back?"

"I wish I could honestly say no, but I can't. I won't lie to you, there is every chance he may come back."

"Well that settles it. Diane, I want you out of here. Go stay with your sister for a while. I don't want you around here."

"Well what about you? Who will protect you?"

"Mr. and Mrs. Duncan, I can't say he won't come back, but I can't say he will, either. What I can do is place all of you into protective custody. I can have police surrounding your home, and no one would be the wiser."

Diane looked at Brad with a frightened look on her face. He knew it would take a long time before she could forget what she saw in the bedroom. It wouldn't be easy for anyone to forget. She was still shaking as he held her close, trying his best to comfort her.

"I think we would all feel a lot better if the police were nearby. Go ahead and place your men."

"Thank you. I'll have them here pronto."

James went back to the station and talked to a detective friend of his. In no time, the arrangements were made and the Duncan's would be safe. He really wanted this guy before anyone else was hurt.

The next morning, the incident at the Duncan home was on the news, but no mention of police protection. Rebecca was listening while she was getting ready for work and her heart began to pound. She stopped what she was doing to sit down and listen to the broadcast. The phone rang; it was Paula wanting to know if she had been listening. Rebecca told her she was watching the news, then cut the conversation short. She wanted to leave early so she could talk to Mr. Duncan and would talk to her at lunch. The only good thing about this attempt was the killer couldn't follow through and the Duncan's were still alive. Rebecca pulled in the parking lot about eight forty-five, shortly after Mr. Duncan pulled in his space. Within seconds, she was near his car waiting for him.

He told her how frightening this entire experience was, that he was thankful to be alive, and if it had not been for Diane walking in when she did, he might not be here right now. What he didn't talk about was the police protection. No one was to know about that, and it could end up defeating the purpose of catching this insane criminal. Brad assured Rebecca everything was fine. It was time to open the bank soon and he told her not to worry about a thing. That was easier said than done. Soon the bank was open and the tellers at their stations. The bank was crowded and everyone was busy. A man approached Rebecca's station. He claimed to be friends with Wes.

"Hi, I would have been in sooner, but it was difficult, so I thought I would stop in now while I have the courage. I don't know if you remember me. My name is Chuck, a friend of Wes. He uses to talk about you a great deal. I wanted to tell you how sorry I am and if there is anything I can do, please call me. Here is my card; I mean this. He loved you so much and as his friend, I'd like to do whatever I can to help. He was like a brother to me."

"Thank you. I do remember you. He talked about you a lot too, thank you. I appreciate your offer, but you really don't have to do this. I'll be fine, really."

"Under different circumstances, I'm sure you would be, but with a sick killer out there… well, please call me anytime. I mean that."

Once again she thanked him and cashed his check so he could be on his way. She did agree to call if she needed him, although she couldn't imagine why. Never the less, the offer was very sweet. The morning went by quickly. Lunchtime arrived and Rebecca went out to meet Paula. They met at the diner across the street. She was telling Paula all about Chuck and what happened to the Duncan's. There was plenty to keep them talking through lunch. Suddenly, she noticed someone walking toward them. It was Chuck.

"Good afternoon ladies, enjoying your lunch?"

"Hello Chuck, yes we are. I'd like you to meet my best friend, Paula. She's always there when I need her; she's the greatest."

"Why hello, Paula, it's nice to meet you. I'm...I was a close friend of Wes; he's very well missed. Did you know him?"

"Yes I did. Has Rebecca told you we are best friends? In fact, my fiancé was also killed, just before Wes. The four of us use to go out together sometimes."

"Oh yes, he did mention that a few times. From what he told me, all of you had great times together. I'm sorry for your loss. Wes and Bill were great guys."

"He talked about Bill?"

"Well, not really talk about him, just mentioned a few times. Well, I really should be going. You ladies have a great day and maybe I'll even see you around again."

"So, what do you think?"

"I'm not sure. How well do you know him?"

"Not as well as I know you, but he seems like a nice enough guy."

"Well, I'll take your word for it. Don't forget, today after work we scheduled makeovers. Stop and pick me up. I get off at five. See you then."

The beauty salon was packed. Rebecca and Paula were almost finished and feeling on top of the world. They were surprised when they walked out the door and found Chuck waiting for them.

"May I buy you two beautiful ladies a drink?"

"Chuck, that's very sweet of you, but Paula and I planned tonight a ladies' night out. You know, girl things."

"I understand, maybe another time."

"Chuck, listen, you're a great guy, but you don't have to play my keeper. I'm fine really. If there's anything I do need you for, I promise to call. OK?"

"I understand, and I don't mean to be a pest. I just want to look after you like I know Wes would have. Please accept my apologies."

"We accept, and like I said, if I do need anything, I will call. I appreciate your gesture, but don't waste your time looking after me when you could be out on a date. Thank you and take care."

He nodded in agreement, then walked away. The girls stopped for a drink before going home.

"Rebecca, are you sure he can be trusted? He's kind of spooky if you ask me. I mean, it could be my imagination running away with me after everything that's happened, but he does make my stomach churn."

"I believe he's harmless. He's just acting as a good friend, like he thinks Wes would want him to. Nothing more."

They walked around and did some shopping, as well as window shopping. They each found an outfit they just had to have. Rebecca found a few baby items that were too cute to pass up, while Paula found the most adorable christening outfit. It would work for a male or female. An announcement was being made that the store was closing soon, warning shoppers to finish and go to the checkout. The next day at work, Brad asked Rebecca to step into his office.

"I called you in here to ask a favor of you. Diane is still upset about what happened the other day. I'd like to get her mind off that incident, and I was wondering if you don't have any plans for tonight, would you come over for dinner?"

"Thank you, but do you think that's a good idea? I wouldn't want her to feel pressured."

"On the contrary when we have company, she's much more relaxed. It would be good for her and take her mind off things."

"Well, if you're sure, I'd love to come. Thank you."

"Your friend is welcome as well. Please bring her along."

"I'm sure she would love to, thank you again."

Returning to her station, she found a vase of roses. They were from Chuck. When she opened her station, there he was waiting to ask her out to dinner. Again, she asked him to stop and that she already had plans. He wasn't about to leave without a yes for an answer. Brad approached Rebecca, asking her what the holdup was about. She explained what was happening before he warned Chuck not to bother her at work. Brad told him if he had bank business, to take care of it, otherwise he would call security. Finally, he left, leaving her shaken.

"Take ten minutes to calm down, then open your station. Is he going to be a problem for you?"

"I didn't think so, but now I'm not so sure. I've asked him to stop but he's very persistent."

"Don't worry, I'll make sure the guards are aware of this situation and one of them will follow you home to make sure you're safe."

The rest of the day was busy. Rebecca was fine the remainder of the day, not hearing from Chuck. She did feel better having the guard follow her home after the work day was done. He didn't leave until she was inside her apartment door. She made a quick call to Paula about dinner, then took a soak in the tub with a cup of herbal tea was perfect. Paula was very uncomfortable and concerned about Rebecca and talked her into calling James Garrett. At first she didn't think much of it, until she thought about the guard following her home. He couldn't do that every night. Immediately after she hung up with Paula she called James and told him everything. He promised to check him out and get back to her in the morning. A bit an of guilt trip set in and she was hoping she wasn't jumping to conclusions. Rebecca finished dressing. It wasn't long before Paula arrived and they were ready to leave for dinner. She told Paula about her conversation with James, and that he promised to get back with her as soon as he could. By the time they finished the conversation, they had pulled up into the Duncan driveway.

Diane was excited and Brad had planned a simple barbeque for them, just some steaks and potatoes on the grill. During dinner they talked and Diane did seem to forget about what happened. She really seemed to be enjoying herself like Brad said she would. The evening was successfully relaxing to everyone. Morning arrived and James called to let her know he couldn't come up with one negative thing about Chuck, but did warn her to be careful regardless. The rest of the week she hadn't heard, or seen, Chuck. That weekend Brad was called out of town. His grandmother had passed away. Diane never knew his grandmother. For that matter, Brad never really knew her himself. She was upset with Brad's father for some unknown reason, which may never be known. He suggested to Diane that she stay at home. He thought it might be a good idea to call Rebecca and Paula to keep her company for the weekend. A girl's weekend thing. There was no sense in her staying in the house by herself. That evening, Brad was leaving, as Paula and Rebecca were about to knock on the door.

Diane greeted them at the door then showed them into the dining room for tea. Brad kissed his wife goodbye and told the girls to have a great weekend. They talked and talked about so many ideas, of what they could do over the weekend. To start the weekend off, they planned on having dinner out, then maybe some window shopping. Diane suggested pizza. It's been a long time since she's had it, and who doesn't like pizza. They all piled into Diane's car, tuned into some rock and roll music on the radio, and pulled out. It felt like they were reliving their teen years all over again, giggling and singing. Soon they arrived at the Pizza Shack. Ready to go in, Rebecca realized she dropped her wallet in the car. Diane gave her the keys while she and Paula went in to save a seat. When she looked in the car window, there was her wallet on the floor. She unlocked the door and sat in the seat. She leaned over to pick up her wallet. When she tried to stand up, there was Chuck.

"Hello! I was getting in my car when I looked up and saw you over here. I thought I would come over and say hi. Is anything wrong?"

She was nervous, but tried her best not to let him see that; it would give him an edge. Unfortunately, they were the only ones in the parking lot.

"Chuck, listen. I told you if I needed you for anything, I would call you. Why are you pressing me?"

"You don't understand; I just want to be your friend. Why won't you let me be your friend?"

"You're making me feel very uncomfortable. Would you be doing this if Wes were still alive?"

"He isn't though, is he?"

He moved closer towards her. She asked him to move away before she screamed, but he pushed her back in the car. Rebecca began screaming, until he covered her mouth. Her fear grew more intense as she struggled. She was pregnant and did not want to lose this baby. Chuck yelled for her to stop. He didn't want to hurt her. He began moving even closer, still. He never noticed her reaching in her purse to pull out her keys. She poked him in his eyes, pushing him away with her foot, and leaning on the horn with her hand. Almost immediately James rushed over to help. Forcing him face down to the ground, he cuffed his hands. Diane and Paula ran out in time to see him ready to take Chuck away.

"I just happen to stop in to pick up something for dinner when I heard the horn. Lucky I did."

"I can't thank you enough."

She looked at Chuck in great disappointment.

"Why? Why did you do this? What kind of friend are you? If Wes were here…he would tear you apart with his bare hands."

"Then I suppose that would make me lucky."

James took Chuck by the arm to his car and took him to the station. Paula and Diane fussed over Rebecca for a while. After a few minutes, she finally calmed down. They had to talk her into having dinner. They ordered some wine to help calm her nerves. By the end of dinner, she was fine. They went out to go window shopping, then stopped for ice cream on the way home. In the back was a family celebrating their son's birthday. The table was filled with presents and they were singing happy birthday. The mother was taking pictures while the little boy blew out the candles. Rebecca stared for a while, wondering what it would be like for her and her baby someday. Diane and Paula noticed the smile on her face; it couldn't have been more obvious what was on her mind. All of this gave Diane the idea to give her a baby shower. What a great idea! Later they arrived at Diane's and found James waiting for them. He didn't like having to tell her they had to let him go. His high priced fancy lawyer got him off. It wasn't something James enjoyed telling anyone, any more than Rebecca would want to hear about this. He brought along restraining papers for her to sign. It was the best he could do for her under the circumstances, along with an apology. The girls were appalled, but Rebecca did sign the papers. They went inside.

"Are you alright?"

"I'm fine, Diane, thank you. I suppose I just have to have faith in the judicial system. What else can I do? I know I won't jeopardize my baby for this nonsense. I'll never have another chance to have Wes's baby."

Diane locked the door behind them, leading them into the living room. They were going to make a slumber party out of what was left of the night. Paula helped Diane make popcorn and pour soft drinks. Rebecca was in the room looking through Diane's movie collection, and making sure they had plenty of tissues. It wasn't long before they were watching a movie, forgetting about what happened that evening. They laughed, giggled, and cried; it was nearly three in the morning when they were all asleep.

Nine fifteen the next morning, Brad called to check on all of them. Diane told him everything that had happened. None of them were thrilled about Chuck being released, but they're hoping the restraining order will help. At least for the weekend, Rebecca would be safe with police surrounding the house. The girls decided to stay; there was plenty to keep them entertained. In the back, the Duncan's had a huge swimming pool and a game room downstairs. They could cook on the grill for dinner. After last night, Diane and Paula thought it would be best for Rebecca to relax and not have to worry about Chuck following them. Rebecca made breakfast for them, serving it on the patio. It was a beautiful morning and the gentle breeze kissed their faces as they enjoyed their coffee. Diane brought up the idea of a baby shower, but Rebecca thought it was premature to plan anything like that now.

"It's never too early. Time passes quickly, and before you know it, that little bundle of joy will be here."

"That's scary. I'm not even sure I will make a good mother. It's not like I've ever taken care of a baby before. I never even baby-sat before."

"Well, there's one thing you can be sure of, you always make your best mistakes with your first child, but you learn as you go along. Your motherly instincts will guide you. Besides, Paula and I will be here for you anytime you need us, so you won't be alone."

"Diane is right. You'll make a great mother."

They talked for a while; played some cards. By noon, they were ready for a swim. Splashing and laughing all afternoon, they had lost track of time. They didn't realize what time it was until the phone rang. James Garrett wanted to check on them, especially Rebecca, after her ordeal last night. Diane knew he was just outside the house, so she invited him in to join them for dinner. He graciously declined, said he had a prior engagement, but he was really spending every moment he could working on this case. The town was terrorized and he wanted to put an end to everyone's fear. He thanked her, then asked to tell Rebecca to be very careful if she went out.

His shift was over, but he went back to the station to look over the files. There just had to be some connection between these murders, probably something staring right at him, and for whatever reason, it's not catching his eye. The chief of police happened to walk by James's office, watching him hover over files scattered on his desk.

"James, you can't be getting much rest. I know that, because I know when you're on duty, and you're here all the time afterwards. I know you want to catch this guy, believe me, we all do, but wearing yourself down isn't the way. You can't remain focused, or function as well as you should, if you're not getting your rest, so go home. "

"I understand what you're saying, sir, but really, I'm fine. There's no need to be concerned I won't get any rest thinking about these files, so I might as well be here going over them."

"Lieutenant, don't make me pull rank. I will if I have to, so why don't you just go on home. You're one of our best men, and I'd like to keep it that way."

"Yes, sir. Alright, you win, I'll go home."

James left. But just like he told the chief, he couldn't stop thinking about this case. Maybe his chief was right, maybe he did need a rest to freshen his memory. James was the type of cop who when he started a case, he couldn't let go until it was solved, not to mention he didn't want to see anyone else killed. When he arrived home, he ran a hot tub, hoping to sink in and let his mind drift from this case, if that were at all possible. He undressed and stepped into the tub, immersing himself into the hot water. He tried to let go of everything on his mind, and for a while he did, but then questions whirled through his head like a tornado. Bill and Wes, the crime scenes…in his head, he could see them in their bed with an ax in their chest, as if it were a few minutes ago.

The killer didn't slip up yet, but he will. They all do, and when he does, James planned on being the one to catch him. He stepped out of the tub, drying himself, when he heard a noise. He put on his robe, then carefully looked out in his bedroom, all around, and at the window. No one was there. He removed his gun from his nightstand and quietly walked towards the living room, ready to shoot. It was difficult to see in the dark, and the rain was pouring, beating against the windows. One window in the living room was open, where the noise was coming from. The shutters were banging. As he closed the window, he turned around. There was a loud crack of thunder. The brightness from the lightening flashed long enough for James to see a figure standing before him with an ax, ready to come down on him. James aimed his gun. As he shot, he found himself sitting up in bed, dampened in perspiration. His heart pounding like a drum, he realized it was all a bad dream. Thank God for that. Then again, if it had been real, all this would be over with. The alarm clock was still ringing. He reached over, slamming his hand to turn it off, then fell back down on the bed to catch his breath.

He sat on the edge of his bed, again, going over details in his head. Coffee seemed like a good idea, so he rose from his bed and into the kitchen to brew a pot. He showered, shaved, and dressed, and went back into the kitchen. When he looked in the living room, he noticed the window was open. When he walked over to close it, he saw the ground was dry. The phone rang, as he was about to pour some coffee. It was homicide calling to tell him there was another murder last night.

"I'm on my way. I want you to go over that place with a fine toothcomb! Don't miss a thing. I don't care how trivial you think it may be, go over it anyway. I should be there in fifteen minutes."

While driving over, what was on his mind was, after seven years of being on the force, this was a part of his job he could never get used to. How does anyone get used to such brutality? He only hopes there will be some kind of clue this time. When he arrived at the scene, an officer approached him with a piece of evidence that could lead to an arrest.

"This just can't be! Where did you get this?"

"I'm sorry, Lieutenant. We found it on the floor next to the victims bed. Is something wrong?"

James walked past him and into the house. He approached the sergeant, telling him he wanted a report ASAP sent to his office. He started looking around, hoping to find something else. He was there for thirty minutes before he gave up. Torn between anger and disbelief, he left the house and sped off in his car. How could this be? This was too easy. The whole thing smelled of a set up, and all he had to do was prove it, somehow. It wasn't long before he parked in front of the Duncan home, took a deep breath and started up, the pathway, walking slower as he approached the door. He stood for a moment, still thinking something about this isn't right. However, he had no choice. He had to do his duty and uphold the law. As he raised his hand to knock, Diane answered the door.

"Well, this is a surprise! Won't you come in, Lieutenant?"

"Thank you. Is Rebecca available?"

"Why, yes she is. Give me a moment and I'll get her for you."

Diane went to get her; she and Paula were busy in conversation.

"Rebecca, the lieutenant is here to see you. I think he's interested in you."

"Why do you say that?"

"Well, because he came here asking for you. Why else would he be here?"

The three ladies went to greet James, only being interested is not the impression she was struck with. He had a serious expression on his face.

"Rebecca Travis, you're under arrest for the murder of Chuck Abrams."

"What! Lieutenant, you don't know what you're saying. Rebecca has worked for my husband a very long time, she's like family. Besides, she's been here with Paula and me the entire weekend."

"Alright, can you testify that she was here all through the night? Never leaving?"

"Well, of course. She was here, with us. Both of them have been here all weekend."

"Can you tell me where she was between one and three AM?"

"Of course, she was in bed. We all were."

"Did you see her in bed between those hours?"

"Well, I didn't go in her room to check on her, if that's what you mean."

"How about you, Miss Lived? Did you see her sleeping in bed between those hours?"

"This is ludicrous! We were all sleeping during that time."

"So, you're saying you did not see her in her bed between those hours?"

Paula and Diane looked at each other and nodded their heads no. As painful as it was for them, Rebecca still understood.

"Lieutenant, what proof do you have that she is the one who killed Chuck last night?"

He held up the bag with a bracelet in it, engraved TO REBECCA FROM WES, I WILL ALWAYS LOVE YOU.

"That is my bracelet, how did you get that?"

"It was found next to the victims bed. I'm sorry, Miss Travis, you'll have to come with me."

"Sweetie, don't you worry. I'll have my lawyer on this and we'll get you out before the day is over."

Diane was determined to keep Rebecca out of prison. There is no way anyone could ever convince her that she's the murderer. Paula was concerned about Rebecca's pregnancy, what affect this would have on her, but Diane reassured her everything would be fine. Immediately, she called Brad to inform him. He advised her to call the lawyer and he would be home as soon as he could. Paula stood by the front door in tears as James escorted Rebecca to his car, reading her rights. Rebecca did her best to hold back the tears, making James very uncomfortable. He couldn't even glance over at her, much less look her straight in the eye. The station wasn't far away, but the drive seemed liked it was taking forever to get there. When they arrived, he turned Rebecca over to Officer O'Leary for finger printing and photo shots. It was more and more difficult for her to hold back the tears, but she had to try her best. Officer O'Leary showed Rebecca to her cell, where James was waiting for her.

"I'm so sorry! I really am truly sorry."

"Then let me go! You know I didn't kill anyone."

"I believe you, but it doesn't look good for you. What evidence I have all leads back to you. I don't have a choice. I wish I did, but I don't. Diane contacted their attorney. Men like Duncan have great lawyers. You'll probably be out on bail in no time. Until then, hang in there. I'm going to do everything I can to clear your name."

James stood up. Leaving her cell, he turned and gave her a comforting smile. Rebecca was feeling very uncomfortable, but scared more than anything. She couldn't force a smile if she wanted. Now she was alone, she did shed some tears. James wasn't so far away that he couldn't hear her crying. This made him more determined to find the real culprit. His gut instinct told him there is no way Rebecca could have done such a deed. As he walked in the office, O'Leary approached him, letting him know the Duncan's lawyer was there to bail out Rebecca. James acknowledged him then went back to his office. Something didn't sit right with him, this is way too easy. It felt more like a set up, but who would want to set her up for murder?

The police were able to get a plaster of the footprints outside the windows of Bill and Wes. What they had from that was it had to have been a man about one hundred and eighty pounds. That would clear Rebecca of Bill and Wes, but Chuck was another issue all together. There were no footprints around Chuck's apartment, there was no grassy ground area, it was all concrete. The bracelet was all they had to go on, not even a fingerprint. Now if she really did do this, how could she be so careless as to lose her bracelet, yet not leave a fingerprint anywhere? She wouldn't go to all the trouble of wearing gloves then losing her bracelet. The real killer is being very careful, but then lost a bracelet? It doesn't make sense, everything was clean, not even torn fabric to be found. Clearly someone is trying to frame Rebecca and James was not going to stop until he put an end to this madness.

He needed to talk to Diane and Paula, knowing full well he wouldn't receive a warm welcome, but he had to talk to them in spite of everything. Getting them to understand why he arrested Rebecca would be a miracle, but maybe there has to be some way they could help clear her name. Again he found himself knocking on Diane's door.

"Lieutenant! Is there something I can do for you?"

"This should explain everything."

He handed her a letter written in Rebecca's handwriting, giving James permission to search through her belongings. Diane grew angry, then looked up at him, giving him a look that could burn right through him.

"You say you're on her side! This tells me you're not. If you truly believe her, you wouldn't be putting her through all this. "

"On the contrary, I'm hoping to find nothing, and in order to do that, I have to search through her things."

Paula was nearby and heard every word spoken before she burst into the room.

"How dare you come back here wanting to search through her things! Haven't you put her through enough already? Get out! Get out this instant."

"It's no use, Paula, he has written consent from Rebecca. Follow me."

"There must be something. Can't we get your attorney here? There has to be something wrong with all this, all he wants to do is send her to prison. I, for one, will not let him do that."

"Paula, we won't either. We're going to fight to clear her name, but don't you see, if we refuse him going through her things, that will make her look guilty. He does have her consent, so it's better if we let him look around."

'Maybe you're right, but I don't trust him."

"We have to; we have no choice. Go on Lieutenant, here is where she stayed."

He followed Diane to the room where she was staying, but she never let him alone there, even for a second. James began searching through the closet, drawers, anything he could look through. He didn't want to leave even one stone unturned. He pulled her suitcase out from underneath the bed, going through that. For a moment, he paused. Removing a pen from his pocket, he gently lifted a scarf with blood on it from the case, putting it in a plastic bag. Diane was flabbergasted and couldn't believe what she saw. Standing there, her entire body went numb, as the color drained from her face. Paula walked in ready to yell and scream but noticed Diane looking as though she saw a ghost.

When she looked at James with a bag in his hand, she asked what was going on and what was in the bag.

"Paula, he found that scarf in Rebecca's case, stained with blood. "

"How do you know he didn't plant it there. It's been known to happen."

"I watched his every move, he didn't plant it there. There just has to be an explanation. There has to be."

Paula walked over to look at the scarf he found.

"There is an explanation. When Rebecca and I were packing to come over, I broke a glass in her room, just before I fell. When I did fall the glass cut my leg and she used her scarf to wrap my leg. If you don't believe, me see for yourself."

She lifted her dress high enough for James to see the cut.

"That's a bad cut, did you go to the emergency room to have it checked?"

"No, it looks worse than it is. Rebecca cleaned it with peroxide and used an antibiotic cream. It feels fine now. If you want, I can give a sample of my blood to test against the blood on that scarf and you'll see for yourself that I'm telling the truth."

"I'm sorry, but I still have to check this. Ladies, I don't believe she's guilty, but the evidence is against her on this one. I want to find the killer and clear her name. I don't believe she's guilty."

Paula had nothing to say. Diane understood but didn't like it and showed James to the door. As he was leaving, her attorney was walking up the walkway with Rebecca. Diane and Paula were so glad to see her, they hurried out the door to greet her. The three of them hugged and showed great concern for Rebecca.

"Hello, it's good to see you out. I have to go, but you hang in there."

"I'll do my best, but whatever you do, please hurry."

Rebecca and the attorney, Jeff Fanala, went inside to talk to the ladies and try to reassure her.

"Brad won't be home until tomorrow. He called from the hotel where he's staying. I told him I'd handle everything, so none of you have to worry. When he gets back, we'll have a meeting about all this, and we will get your name cleared. I don't see why that would be a problem, you have a record that's as clean as it can be, so I'm sure we'll be fine."

They talked for nearly two hours before he left, and he told them he would keep in touch. Diane offered Rebecca something to eat; she had to have been hungry. Her nerves were restless, so all she really wanted was some tea and a long soak in the tub. Paula thought she might change her mind after a soak, so she and Diane made something light for dinner. They all had hopes that things would work out for everyone.

Back at the station, James received the results from the tests run on the scarf and checked it with the file he kept on Paula. The types matched perfectly. So maybe she was telling the truth. This still left him with nothing to go on other than the victims were all men. There was a question mark next to Wes and Bill's names. Chuck's only reason was he was a pervert. How Brad fit into all this was a mystery, only he was still alive. A good thing, of course, but whoever is killing these men off, could have killed Brad and Diane. Instead, when Diane screamed, he ran off. This is going to be a long night and some heavy duty coffee drinking. Brad arrived home just as Paula and Rebecca were leaving.

"Rebecca, I'm so sorry about everything, I really wanted to be here when you were released; but there was a delay at the airport. How are you doing?"

"I'm fine, really, but thank you. I appreciate all you've done. I just don't know how I'll ever repay you and Diane for everything."

"No need, we all love you and we don't mind doing whatever we can to help. Just be safe."

"I'll see to that. I'm going to take her home and make sure she rests. She has been through so much already."

"Thank you, Paula, but remember you've been through a difficult time yourself."

"Yes, but I'm not pregnant. Rebecca has more of a reason to take care of herself, and I'll see to it that she does. After all, I'm going to be an Aunt."

They all said goodbye before Paula drove Rebecca home. Diane and Brad talked about the weekend and how great it could have been, up until Rebecca was arrested. Now she is out and Jeff would handle things for her. They relaxed in the living room while Brad told Diane about his weekend, mostly business and hardly any rest time. They spent the remainder of the evening together, relaxing on the sofa. They each shared their stories as to what happened with each other over the weekend.

"We can be thankful for Jeff, and I'm sure James is doing his part, but a prayer or two couldn't hurt."

As Rebecca walked up to her apartment door, she inserted the key and unlocked it. Opening the door carefully, she turned on the lights and she stood in her living room, looking around. She is really home, then suddenly she burst into tears. Paula tried to comfort her. She went on to tell Paula how lucky she is, and how awful it was being in jail. She tried to explain to Rebecca that it was all over and she really needed to calm down, for the sake of the baby. The phone rang; it was Louise, Wes's mother. She and Rebecca talked on the phone for at least an hour. What perfect timing. When they were through, Rebecca had calmed down.

"You know, when I lost Wes, it was a very difficult time. Then I found out I was pregnant; I was petrified thinking I'll be all alone raising his baby. Now I see things differently. I have more loved ones around than I could have hoped for. I'm really very lucky."

"We're all here for you. How could you possibly think for even a moment you would be alone. I'll always be here for you, and so will the others."

Before long, they both dozed off on the sofa. It was a very long and tiring weekend.

CHAPTER 4

It was almost one in the morning when James finally decided to go home. He went straight to his car, then unlocked his door. When he looked, there was an ax laying on the front seat. He saw there were words carved on the handle.

BACK OFF

He picked it up carefully, with a napkin that was on his dashboard. He went back to the station to have it dusted for fingerprints. He wasn't about to leave until the results came back. While he waited, he went back to his office with some coffee, looking over the files again. When the results were back, this didn't take long at all, there were no prints on the ax. Not on the handle, or the blade. Never the less, he bagged it and locked it in his desk drawer before he left. This guy was really ticking him off. James would stop at nothing until he was found. When he was back home, he poured himself a drink, then soaked in a hot, steamy tub. He still couldn't take his mind off this case. When he was through, he toweled off, and put on some shorts sitting on the edge of his bed with what was left of his drink. He looked up and noticed there was a figure standing outside his window, looking in at him.

James pulled his gun from his nightstand drawer and was ready to shoot, but he was gone! Quickly as he could, he slipped into his pants then leaped through the window to chase him. There was no one in sight. Across the street was a pickup truck, so he rushed over as quietly as he could, but there was no one there, either! This couldn't be, it was as if he vanished into thin air! James went back, climbing through his window, and locking it. He turned to find a note on his bed.

UNLESS YOU WANT TO JOIN THE OTHERS, BACK OFF PIG.

Looking at the letter, he realized how clever this heartless, good for nothing really is. He never cut out the letters and pasted them from a magazine, it wasn't handwritten. He actually stenciled this note. If he went to all this trouble for the note, chances are there would be no fingerprints. Maybe he was counting on that. Either way, James would have this checked for prints also. He couldn't remain on a lucky streak forever, he had to slip up sometime. Now it was clear, he wanted James off this case, which was never going to happen. It was now almost three A.M. He decided to try and get a few hours' sleep, anyway. Quietly, he lay in bed, trying his best to get some sleep. His mind was struggling with this case, and what happened tonight. The attack on James did make sense; obviously someone wanted him off this case. The crime scenes, files, all of it, kept rushing through his head. With the exception of Chuck, Bill and Wes worked different jobs, so it couldn't have been work related. Maybe it had to do with Paula and Rebecca, but no one threatened their lives, thank God. Except, Chuck did try to harm her, but not kill her. Something, somewhere had to connect. James rolled over on his side and there he was, the ax was about to drop. The alarm went off. James sat up screaming, realizing it was all a bad dream. He hit the clock with his fist, then went in the bathroom to splash water on his face. Like every morning, he went for a thirty-minute jog then came back and showered. He dressed, poured some juice while looking over the note he found on his bed last night. Something else to add to his files.

Paula is at work unloading a shipment of stock with her manager, Kyle Langdon. He notices something is not quite right and approaches her. He suggested a coffee break so they could have a moment to talk, but all she wants to do is keep busy. She had been pushing herself hard lately. His concern was it either helped relieve her frustrations, or she was headed for a break down. Throughout the day, she was working herself hard, but never neglected the customers. That part was a strain for her, but did her best. Kyle had to order her to take a lunch, much less a break. It wasn't difficult to understand the frustration she and Rebecca were going through, and had every right to do so, but he didn't want to see her make herself sick. Paula spent a lot of time near the register and pricing merchandise. He felt completely helpless.

"Paula, I have to make a deposit at the bank. Will you be alright until I get back?"

"I'll be fine. You go on ahead and don't worry about a thing, after all, I had a great teacher."

"Thank you, but didn't you just get a raise?"

"Oh, go on, I'll be fine."

At least if nothing else, she was smiling. After returning her smile, he turned, leaving the shop, closing the door behind him. He didn't really have a deposit to make, he just wanted to check on Rebecca and talk to Brad. They were friends all through school, always confiding in each other when the other had a problem. When he arrived at the bank and went inside, Brad saw him and immediately went to greet him.

"Kyle, it's always good to see you. Is this business or pleasure?"

"A little of both, but nothing to do with bank business, at least half of what I came here for. Can we talk in private?"

"I understand. Why don't we go in my office, I just made some fresh coffee?"

They talked for a while, and unfortunately, Rebecca wasn't much better than Paula. They were both a wreck, but trying their best. They talked a few more minutes than Kyle had to get back to his shop.

James was in his office studying the files when the chief walked in to speak with him.

"James, I don't know if you're aware yet, but there was another incident at the Duncan home last night. This time, it was close. You better get over there fast."

James jumped up out of his seat, ran out the door, and slapped his light on the roof of his car, driving as quickly as he could to get there. This is the second time he went after Brad, but still did not kill him. Is he playing games now, or what reason is there behind this? Maybe a distraction for the real thing. Somehow he would find out. When he arrived, he ran up the walkway, then straight into the house. Brad and Diane were on the sofa, Diane in tears. O'Leary approached James, filling him in. This time he was alone. The ax came bursting through the window and in the back of the sofa, just missing Brad within inches. Diane looked up and noticed James was in the room.

"So, when are you going to find this maniac? Next time, he just may succeed killing my husband. Are you going to catch him before or after my husband is killed?"

"Mrs. Duncan, I'm doing my best. So far, we still have no prints on anything. This guy is slick. We're working day and night to find him and put him away for good."

"I certainly hope it's before, and not after something happens to my husband, otherwise, I may be forced to press charges."

"Diane, please."

"Please what, Brad? Three men are dead, and he claims Rebecca is a suspect, a pregnant woman. Who will you blame next, the dog across the street?"

"Diane, please make some coffee for us. We could use a break."

"Don't you dare try to justify him, not after all he's done."

Reluctantly, she did as Brad asked. Maybe she would even calm down some before she came back in the room. The men talked, but Brad really didn't know much. His back was facing the window so he couldn't see anyone. When James felt he had all he could get, he left before Diane came back. He didn't want to upset her any more than he already had. It wasn't intentional, but it was understandable. When he was in his car, he called the chief, Craig, to fill him in on what he had. This time it was too close and Craig assigned more men on this case, anyone he could spare. At least with Chuck there was a possible motive, but it didn't fit the others. Certainly he didn't believe for one minute that Rebecca could do this, not even for a second. Something just had to break and soon. Later that day, he briefly stopped at Rebecca's apartment after she was home from work, to check on her. She wanted to know why he would even stop in to see her. He paused for a moment, then saw she had a concerned look on her face.

"Are you alright?"

"Mr. Duncan didn't come in to work today. He never misses, not even one day since I've been there. I hope nothing is wrong."

"Maybe he decided to take the day off. He's been there quite a while. He might just need a break."

"In all the time I've known him, he has never taken even one day off."

"Rebecca, all of you have been through an awful lot of stress. This might be the time for him to change his mind about taking a day off."

"I'll go along with that, only because I'd like to think that you're right. Then again, maybe I can find out for sure."

She was ready to call Diane at home, but James stopped her. He decided he might as well fill her in.

"What's going on? I want to know right now, and do not tell me you don't know, because I refuse to accept that."

"Wait a minute, slow down."

"Mr. Duncan wasn't at work today, so don't play dumb I want answers now."

"Alright, I'll tell you, but you cannot tell another sole."

"Oh my God, is he..."

"No, he's not dead, but there was another attempt on his life."

"I knew something was wrong when he didn't come in today."

"Rebecca, listen to me. He's fine, I promise you that. He is shaken up, and with good reason. I'm not going to rest until I find this jerk and lock him up for what's left of his miserable life. I promise you, I will catch him. Brad is fine I'm sure."

"Really! Do you know what it's like to have an attempt made on your life? Do you?"

"I'm a cop, believe me, I know."

Rebecca hung her head in despair. She felt terrible about what she said to him.

"I'm sorry. The stress from everything that's happened the past few months are getting to me. I don't understand any of this, or even why it's happening."

"No one understands why this is happening. One thing for sure is, you need to take care of yourself. You don't want to get so upset that you risk losing this baby. Let us handle this and you take care of you, O.K.?"

Looking over his shoulder, she saw Paula drive up. Rebecca closed her door and walked to the curb with James. She thanked him then sat in the car with Paula. James stood there until they were in the car and driving off safely before he turned walking in the opposite direction.

"So, what did he want? Hasn't he caused enough trouble already?"

"He just stopped by to check on me and to apologize. He genuinely seems to be sorry about arresting me."

"I still think you should be careful where he's concerned. It's his job to be tricky, and he may try to trick you."

"I don't think so, but I will be careful, I promise."

Paula was driving and didn't tell Rebecca where they were going. Rebecca noticed she was pulling in the lot for the park. She stopped near a picnic bench where they could just sit, relax, and talk away the day's stress. It was beautiful, trees everywhere and the duck pond nearby. The ducks waddled up to anyone who would feed them. It was a peaceful place; the only sounds were natures. They walked on the path for maybe two miles before they even realized dusk was beginning to set and decided it was time to leave. On the way they stopped to check on Brad and Diane. Rebecca was so glad to see they were safe, then they left to go home.

In the morning, as Rebecca was leaving for work, she found reporters outside her door, making it impossible for her to get past them. They knew she was friends with the Duncan's and wanted information as to what had happened. She had no choice but to go back in her apartment and lock the door. Immediately, she called James at the station to fill him in on what was happening. He told her to sit tight and he would be there shortly. Craig just happened to be there when the call came in for James.

"So, what was that about?"

"Rebecca was on her way to work, but because of the reporters outside her door, she's trapped in her apartment. They want information about what had happened at the Duncan's."

"How in the hell did they find out about that?"

"I don't know, yet, but I will find out."

James jumped in his car and sped to Rebecca's place. It was ridiculous, reporters swarming all around. They were like vultures waiting and screaming for her to come out and talk to them. He called for the black and whites to come clear them out, and arrest them if needed. James made a brief announcement to them before they arrived, telling them at this time the police are not ready to make this public. When they were, the press would be alerted, then ordered them away just as the men in blue arrived. He knocked on Rebecca's door to let her know who he was so she would let him in; they would have to wait awhile until the police cleared them out. Then he would escort her to work to make sure she wouldn't be harassed by reporters. He would come back after her shift and see to it she made it home. As he pulled out, he noticed a car in his rearview mirror that looked familiar. He saw that car when the reporters were at her apartment. He pulled over so that he would still be able to catch up with Rebecca if he indeed was a reporter. He watched as the owner of the car stepped out and began to approach her. He stepped out of his car and made a move on him. He nabbed the reporter, as he was about to speak to Rebecca, then warned him off. She noticed what was happening, but James motioned for her to go inside. They both went back to their cars as James waited for him to leave. The reporter left, but James drove around the block and came back just to be sure he left for good.

The remainder of the day was pretty quiet, until James was ready to leave for the bank. A call came in for him. It was Rebecca and she was hysterical. O'Leary had taken the call as James was listening, then said he would take this one. He raced over to her apartment to find out what may have happened. He was supposed to follow her home.

"Rebecca, I thought I was going to meet you after work?"

"I realize that, but I wasn't feeling well, so I left early. I didn't want to monopolize your time; I know you're very busy."

"You should have called me, what's happening?"

"I think it's best if you see this for yourself."

She told him to go into her bedroom. She couldn't go in there. When he walked in, he found an ax in a pillow with a message taped to the handle.

YOU'RE CARRYING A DEMON BABY, YOU'RE ONLY

SAFETY IS TO ABORT.

Rebecca couldn't even go into her room; she couldn't believe any human could be this devastatingly cruel. James left the room to check on Rebecca.

"This is getting way more serious than when this started. I want you out of town immediately, do you understand?"

"What about my job?"

"I'm sure if we talked to Brad he would understand, and probably even agree with me. There's only one way to find out, let's go."

"Lieutenant, there is no…"

"Catch me back at the station, we'll talk then."

The Ax

He drove Rebecca to the Duncan home and they all sat down to discuss what happened. Diane and Brad fussed over her for a while, then decided James was right. Brad called Jeff for his assistance since Rebecca was out on bail. There is no way they would let her stay in town. For her own safety, they agreed it would be best if she were out of town. Brad would think of something to tell everyone at the bank, but Rebecca needed to be safe.

"Jeff said he would be right over. He wants to get into this now."

"I'll put on some coffee."

As she began to leave the room, she stopped, then slowly turned, looking straight at James.

"Maybe you're not so bad after all. Come with me Rebecca, help me with the coffee. I have a cake we can serve. I just bought it fresh today."

"I told you she would come around. This whole mess has everyone on edge."

"Believe me, I realize that. I want to catch this son of a bitch more than you know."

Jeff had arrived and Brad let him in. They joined James in the living room just as Rebecca brought in the tray with coffee.

"Diane will be right in. She wanted to serve a little something with the coffee."

"I made a few calls before coming over and managed to get approval for her to leave the state, since she will be in my custody. Now, we all have to keep this on a need to know basis. In this case, there will be none. I've been planning a trip to visit my parents in Iowa."

They discussed all the details; everyone was in agreement. Rebecca wanted to let Paula know what was going on, but James told her absolutely no one was to be told of this. She didn't like it since she and Paula are so close, but she played along. The arrangements were made. Rebecca would stay the night, then in the morning, James would take her back to her apartment to pack then drive her and Jeff to the airport. One look at Jeff and no one would dare bother Rebecca. His looks would make any girl melt, but his muscular physic would put fear into anyone even thinking about messing with him. Yet, at the same time, he could be so tender, if the occasion called for it, like now with Rebecca.

The night seemed especially long. She couldn't sleep if her life depended on it. In this case, it was why she couldn't sleep. She moved the chair over to the window then sat there gazing at the stars in the sky. It was incredible how her life has changed in the past few months. This is not the way she had hoped her life would turn out. If this is one of life's surprises, it was not a good one. Well, then again, the baby is the only good surprise out of all this. All these thoughts going through her head made her sleepy. It was a kind of sleepy that was really relaxing, and thoughts of the baby made her forget her troubles and plan for the arrival until she went to sleep.

By morning, when Diane came in to wake her, she found Rebecca sleeping in the chair. She gave her a nudge when Rebecca opened her eyes.

"Did you sleep all night in this chair?"

"No, not really. I had a difficult time trying to sleep so I was looking out the window and thinking about everything, I guess I just drifted off to sleep."

"Why don't you get a few more hours of sleep before James and Jeff arrive. You'll need it for later."

"Thanks, Diane."

Diane left, but Rebecca couldn't get back to sleep. So she showered and dressed in clothes Diane had left for her. They talked for a while and Rebecca expressed her concerns for them. Two attempts on Brad's life had her very concerned. Diane did her best to reassure Rebecca that everything would be fine, and she was to take care of herself. Before long, both James and Jeff arrived, ready to go. They stopped at the apartment to pack then went straight to the airport. Rebecca was quiet the entire time, she had a sick feeling in her stomach making her nauseated, but had nothing to do with the pregnancy. Literally, she was being pushed out of her life; it was for a good reason. What would be next? Having to move away for good. Jeff glanced over at her. He could see how nervous she was and took her hand in his, trying to comfort her. She returned the glance, bothered by it. Jeff is extremely attractive, not to mention, he has quite a physic. At that moment she pulled her hand back and apologized. What was she thinking? His deep voice only added to his charisma.

"I'm sorry, I didn't mean to offend you. I was only trying to comfort you."

"I realize that and thank you, but it's me. I can't believe any of this is happening."

She turned her head looking out the window trying to restrain herself. James parked the car so he could see them off. They checked the luggage then waited until boarding time.

"Rebecca, will you be alright? You look a little pale."

"I hate leaving town without saying goodbye to Paula. We've been through so much together and I don't want her to worry."

"I'll talk to her after your flight takes off, don't worry. I'll take care of the Duncan's too, so please try and relax. The worrying can't be good for the baby or you. I know you want to take special precautions to have a healthy baby."

"Mr. Fanala, I can't thank you enough for all you're doing for me."

"Please, call me Jeff. No thanks are necessary. Like James, I want to put an end to this madness."

It was time to board. Jeff and Rebecca said goodbye to James and said they would be in touch. She couldn't help herself, she had to hug James. She knew he was trying to help. James didn't leave until their flight took off. Once they were in their seats and comfortable, Jeff tried talking to her.

"I can't wait for you to meet my parents. They have a small farm and plenty, of crops; they even have cows. It's not much, but they're happy. My father's dream. Mom got used to it and now loves it herself. It's peaceful, that's probably why they love it so much."

"Did you like living on a farm?"

"Well, my heart was set on being a lawyer, living in the city. Don't get me wrong, I love my parents and the farm is a great little get away when I need one. It's just not for me. How about you?"

"My dreams were altered by that maniac. Since I was a little girl, I use to dream about being a wife, mother, and having a home of my own. Now I wonder if I'll ever have a complete dream come true."

Talking about her dreams wasn't easy, especially since she lost Wes. At least she would still have a part of him, that part is growing inside her, only being alone to raise the baby was not part of her dream. Now she would have to do her best to cope, she was a firm believer in not being given any more than she could handle. Even though at times it was difficult even for her to believe. Now she had to believe it would all work out. After all, now she would have a life counting on her. Jeff is a great comfort to her, but all she really wanted was for everyone to go back to their normal lives again.

The plane was about to land; the trip wasn't long at all. The instant they stepped off the plane, his parents were there waiting to meet them. They were all very happy to see each other, appearances would seem as though they hadn't seen each other in years.

"You must be Rebecca. Jeff has told us so much about you. I'm April and this is my husband, Don. We want you to be comfortable so if there is anything at all we can do, just let us know. No matter how trivial you may think it is, we want you to feel at home."

"Well, Jeff, how about we get going? your mother went all out for lunch. You know your mother."

While the men loaded the station wagon, April was talking to Rebecca. They had a wonderful chat and soon she was feeling so much better. Jeff and his parents were great and they really care about people. This trip may turn out to be a good thing after all. His parents seem like wonderful people.

CHAPTER 5

James stopped in to talk to Paula, letting her know about Rebecca. Of course she was very upset, and it almost took thirty minutes to calm her down and make her realize it was for her own good. Everything was upsetting her and she needed some time away from it all. Paula didn't like it, but she did understand. He offered to take her out to dinner. She agreed and he told her he would pick her up the minute the shop would close. They were close friends and he thought with Rebecca out of town, she could use the company. As he left, he bumped into a friend of his from California, Lewis Turner.

"Lewis, it's great to see you! How have you been?"

"I'm great, it's good to see you. So has some charming lady tied you down yet?"

"No, I'm still a free man, not that I want to be all my life. Being a cop has a bad effect on women. So, are you visiting?"

"Actually, you wrote so much about this place, I just had to see for myself. So far, I like what I see, I'm thinking about moving my practice here."

"Well, it will be great to have you around."

They talked for a while when Lewis noticed Paula in the window of the shop. James saw he was looking at her when he realized Lewis wasn't paying attention.

"She is very beautiful, is she your girlfriend?"

"My girlfriend? No, she's someone going through a difficult time right now both her and her friend. I just stopped by to talk to her a moment."

"That's too bad, she's too beautiful to be alone."

"She wasn't until her boyfriend was killed."

"That's terrible! What happened?"

"I'm not so sure I want to tell you after you came to see our town, and after all I wrote to you about it…on second thought, he was killed with an ax delivered to his chest. There have been several like that, and the only reason I'm telling you all this is I want you to be careful while you're here."

James went on to tell Lewis what has been happening the past few months. His cell phone rang and he had to leave but asked Lewis if they could get together later. Lewis walked in the store to look around when Mr. Langdon offered his assistance. Shaking his head, no, told him if he needed anything, he would let him know and thanked him.

"Paula, I'll be working on the books in my office, if you get busy let me know and I'll be right out."

"Yes, sir."

Lewis walked around looking over all the merchandise in the store, trying to decide what, or if, he wanted anything. He asked Paula if she liked living in the area and that he will be moving around here. She told him she loved living around this area and the people were all very nice. Then she apologized, telling him she would be there if he needed anything, but she had some things to get done. After looking around, he decided on a set of wind chimes, very much like the set his mother had when he was a child. He paid for them and was on his way.

Later that evening, Jeff called James, filling him in on what was happening on his end.

"It's a shame she has to go through all this, she's a terrific woman. Actually, no one should have to go through this."

"No, I agree. By any chance, are you falling for her?"

"Who me? I'm just trying to help her out, that's all."

"She's going through a bad time but she's also still grieving, which makes her very vulnerable. Take it easy with her, OK?"

"Relax, I'm fully aware of all that and I have no intention of doing anything that would hurt her. My family and I are just looking out for her, that's all. Believe me, she'll be fine. We'll take good care of her."

James left to meet with Lewis. He was going to show him around town. At the same time, he was telling him all about the events the past few months and warning him to be very careful, at least until he could solve this case. When James was in the police academy and Lewis was in college, they would toss around some ideas trying to come up with solutions, it was a game back then, but now it's the real thing. Lewis would work the psychotic end while James worked with the actual cases. It wasn't uncommon for a psychiatrist and the police to work together at times. They still had time to catch up on old times and new ones. They stopped at a local bar and grill for a drink, still catching up with each other's lives. James brought up the case again and they talked awhile. Lewis found it interesting, especially that there were no fingerprints, but there was evidence that Rebecca was the killer.

"I'd really like to work with you on this one. Any chance I could have a look at the files?"

"If it will help me put an end to this madness, absolutely. Why don't you meet me in my office tomorrow about nine in the morning?"

"I'll be there. It's getting late. Why don't we call it a night, I'd like to be fresh when I look over those files?"

"Sounds good to me, I could use a little extra sleep. Let me pay the tab and we can go."

They said good night, and again, James warned him to be careful and check his locks. He gave Lewis his card with his number on it, just in case he needed anything.

"Don't worry, if I do I'll call. I'll see you in the morning."

The night was peaceful and long. Just as dawn was breaking, the rooster on the farm began crowing. Rebecca was awakened. A whole new experience for her, she was used to alarm clocks. There was a knock at her bedroom door.

"Come in!"

"Hi, I just wanted to tell you it's alright if you sleep in. You must be exhausted l after everything. I talked to James last night and everything is fine. He asked me to tell you not to worry. So catch up on some sleep and we'll talk later."

"Wait! Jeff, I just wanted to say thank you for everything you've done and I hope I'm not putting anyone out."

"Don't worry, you're not. My folks adore you. Go ahead and get some sleep."

"Thank you, and thank them for me too, please."

She snuggled down in the pillows, closing her eyes as Jeff closed the door. Joining his parents for breakfast, they talked more about what was happening. His mother thought it was awful for her to lose someone then find out later you're about to have his child. She must have been devastated, all though to look at her, you would never know it. She just seemed a bit on edge. Most girls would be hysterical and Jeff explained, for a while, she was, but now she's doing her best to deal with the situation. He told his parents he had some business he had to take care of so he wouldn't be home for lunch.

April and Don both had things to do in town but wanted to stay close to Rebecca.

When she did wake up, she spent her time talking to Jeff's mother. They talked about many things; some of it was about Jeff's childhood. Rebecca sat at the table while April was chopping vegetables and making pies. There was a loud noise that distracted her, causing her to cut her hand. Rebecca wrapped it quickly in a scarf she had on then ran outside looking for Mr. Fanala. He rushed in to check on her. She would have to have some stitches.

"Jeff should be home in about an hour. Make yourself at home. You'll be safe here. If you get hungry, there's food in the icebox. Feel free to help yourself. We'll be back as soon as we get her fixed up. "

Rebecca watched them through the window until they drove out of site. She went into the kitchen to finish what April had started. Certainly she wouldn't feel like it when she came back. When she was through, she cleaned up as best as she could, considering she didn't know where anything belonged. The scenery was beautiful, so she decided to go out and take it all in. Sitting in the rocker and enjoying the relaxation, it was the perfect day and not too hot. Their porch was huge. Aa swing on one end and potted flowers all around. Rose bushes bordered the house and large pots of mums were on either side of the steps. As she was about to close her eyes, a car drove up, it was Jeff. He greeted Rebecca with a smile as he walked up the pathway.

"Hello! I thought you would be keeping my mother company in the kitchen."

"I was, but she cut her hand while chopping vegetables. Your father drove her in to the hospital to have it stitched. They left about forty-five minutes ago."

"Well, then, there would be no sense in going, they'll probably be back shortly. How about some iced tea? Mom makes the best?"

"I'd love some, thank you."

He went inside to pour the tea then joined Rebecca on the porch. When he sat down, he let her know that he had talked to James and everyone is doing fine. They miss her, but they are fine. She offered to make some lunch for him and went inside to find something. Jeff wasn't far behind. He reached for the plates as Rebecca was making sandwiches. Both Jeff and Rebecca turned towards each other, not intentionally they bumped into each other. Momentarily, Jeff held her in his arms while they gazed into each other's eye, no words spoken. When his parents walked in the door, they jumped away from one another. Rebecca pretended like nothing happened and made sandwiches for his parents, while they sat at the table explaining what had happened to Jeff. After lunch the men went outside while the women talked as they were preparing dinner. Rebecca talked about most anything, including the trip she and Paula had taken to the lodge. She described everything in such detail, April said she could almost picture herself there if she closed her eyes. Rebecca couldn't stop thinking about Paula and wondered what she was doing right now.

Diane had stopped in to see how Paula was doing. Of course they were both missing Rebecca, but tried not to think of themselves. She needed this get away after all that has happened. Diane was saying how terrible it was for Rebecca to find that ax when she arrived home. Paula was in shock.

"What ax? James never said anything about finding an ax at her apartment! Are you sure?"

"I'm sorry, maybe he didn't want to worry you. As long as I spilled this much, you might as well know the rest. There was a note with the ax saying her baby was a demon baby and warned her to abort."

"My God, why didn't he tell me this! She is my best friend!"

"Like I said, maybe he didn't want to alarm you. I'm so sorry, I never wanted to upset you; I thought you knew. That was why Rebecca had to go away."

Paula had talked to Mr. Langdon about having the rest of the afternoon. She had to talk to James. Without hesitation, he gave her the rest of the day off. Diane tried to talk her out of it, but there was no stopping her. Rebecca was like a sister to her, so she felt he didn't have a right to keep that information from her. She stormed out of the shop. Diane called ahead to James, to inform him of what happened, giving him a warning to expect her. He planned on meeting her outside to try and talk to her, calmly if at all possible. He stood outside waiting when he heard tires squealing. It was Paula. As quickly as he could, he met her near her car, telling her if she said one word, he would throw her in jail for disturbing the peace. Then had her take a few deep breaths before she spoke.

"What right have you got to keep information about Rebecca from me, you know how important she is to me. Why?"

"That's how she wanted it. She didn't want you to worry, after all, you've been through a lot yourself. I had to respect her wishes; if you really care about, her I would think you would understand that. Tell me something, if you were in Rebecca's place right now and you had to leave, would you want her to know?"

All she could think about was he was right. She would do exactly the same thing. He went on to explain that the only reason Brad and Diane knew was because he drove her there for that night. Everything made sense, not that she liked it any, but she did understand. James told her he has contact with her if need be, and she is fine, not to mention very safe. That is what mattered most, her safety. Paula just wanted to go for a drive; James joined her to keep her company. After an hour she drove to her apartment, inviting James in, and pulled out the pictures of their trip.

"Look at these. We went because we had to. We want to go back again, but not because we have to, because we want to. Can you understand that? You have to find this maniac, we want to come back here again on vacation, can't you understand how close we are? If anything ever happened to her."

"Relax, nothing is going to happen to her, that's why she's out of town, remember? Now I don't know her as long as you have, but I would think she wouldn't want you worrying about her, am I right?"

"Yes, you're right. Alright, I get it, I'll do whatever I have to, but this will be for her."

"I understand. Paula, I promise, I don't know when, but I will put an end to this madness. This is a beautiful place; I can see why the two of you would want to come back. It's getting late, I should be leaving."

"I'm sorry, you'll need a ride back, I'll take you. Thank you for understanding."

Neither of them spoke a word all the way back to the station, but it couldn't have been more clear how Paula was feeling. He realized the promises he made must seem as though they are empty. If only something would break.

"Well, here you are. I know I've been difficult, but Rebecca is my closest and dearest friend. She's like a sister to me and I don't want her hurt."

"I understand, and believe me, I feel the same way. It's understandable that you would think I'm making phony promises, but I do mean what I say, and I won't stop until he's caught."

Paula looked at him and smiled as though to say, I believe you, then drove off. James was about to get in his car and drive home when O'Leary called to him.

"Sorry to bother you, but I have a message for you and I was told to make sure you get this."

James skimmed it over; it was from Lewis. He thanked O'Leary, then called Lewis on his cell phone. Lewis told him he couldn't talk to him on the phone and asked him to come to his home immediately. James told him he would arrive as quickly as he could. Lewis was in his living room looking over a file on his desk when a brick with a note attached smashed through his window. When he went outside to find who had done this, there wasn't a sole anywhere in the street. He went back to read the note, but all it said was:

STAY OUT OF THIS

There was a loud pounding at the door. Lewis looked through the peephole and saw James. He opened the door to let him in, handing him the note. Showing him into the living room, he told James how the note arrived, then let him see the mess. Lewis told him when he went to check it out, there was no one outside.

"Let me get some men over here."

"Never mind that, I need you to look at this file. It may help you with this case."

James sat down and read every detail, then went over it again.

"I don't make it a practice of breaking Doctor patient confidentiality, but this is a special situation and lives are at stake."

When James was finished, he couldn't believe what he read. It just couldn't be possible. Lewis brought him some coffee as they discussed the details. Still in disbelief, James promised to keep this information to himself, unless, of course, he had no choice but to use the information. All he needed now was evidence. He passed on the coffee and thanked Lewi, but he had to leave. He drove home with all this information flooding his brain, almost like a dam breaking. He wanted to tell Jeff but promised he would keep things to himself.

The next morning, Rebecca enjoyed watching the daybreak. The morning sky resembled layers, layers of purple and orange with hints of gold throughout. The sun was huge and orange, almost majestic. She heard the door opening. When she turned her head, she found Jeff poking in to check on her.

"Good morning, you're up early!"

"I'm sorry, I hope I didn't disturb anyone?"

"N, you didn't. I was up working on some paper work when I thought I heard something from your room so I wanted to check on you."

"I'm fine, thank you."

"I know this isn't easy for you, being away from the people you love, and who love you."

"It's alright. I know it's for my own good. Anyway, the time away is wonderful. I didn't realize how wonderful until after we arrived."

"I promise you, you are safe. You know, the scenery is even better from the porch. Would you care to join me?"

They went outside and sat on the swing. He was right it is more beautiful from the porch. Jeff's cell phone vibrated. It was James calling. He excused himself and went inside to talk. When he was through, he rejoined a very concerned looking Rebecca on the porch. Trying to reassure her everything was fine, he went on to tell her James had called to let him know he may have a lead in the case, and this could all be over soon, but he won't be making any promises.

James called Lewis into his office to go over all the files from the beginning to the present. This was the most incredible turn of events James has ever had in all the cases he has ever worked. The problem was finding the evidence to tie it all together. James wanted as much information as he could get from Lewis. In some ways, it made sense, but still didn't seem possible. Lewis was in his office all morning and part of the afternoon, going over details and making plans. James wanted to check on Paula to make sure she was alright but when he called the shop, her manager told him she had called off ill. She had a terrible migraine that made her very sick. It was no wonder, being under all the stress and pressure, then worrying about Rebecca, to top it all off.

James told Mr. Langdon he would stop over and try to talk to her. He suggested to Lew, maybe he could go along. He may be able to help. After a, this is right up his alley.

"I don't know, James, do you think she would mind?"

"I think you are just what she needs. You may be able to convince her to relax, or at least how to handle things. After all, this is your line of work. If anyone can convince her, you should be able to. What do you say?"

"All right, I'll try. That's all I can do."

When they arrived at Paula's, she opened the door. She was in tears.

"Paula, what's wrong? Did something happen?"

"No, it didn't. I just have a migraine and it's killing me. The pain is atrocious; I can't take it anymore."

"Paula, this is my friend, Dr. Lewis, I think he can help you."

"Hello Paula, we met at the shop where you work. Do you remember me?"

"Yes, I do." They sat and talked for a while. Paula told him everything that was on her mind. After an hour or so, Paula's migraine was gone. He prescribed some pills for her in case she had more episodes with the migraines. They are anything, but pleasant. He gave her something to help her sleep before they left and told her he would be available if she needed anything at all. He handed her his card before they left. On their way back to the station, James had an idea. They stopped along the way to check in with Diane and Brad. They had heard from Jeff and Rebecca. She was a little homesick, but was adapting. No more attempts or threats, but they still can't wait for this to be all over with. James drove Lewis back to the station to pick up his car, then he went for a drive. It was getting la, but he wasn't tired. He had too much on his mind. He drove to Peck's Lake to think. What a beautiful area this is. Just ahead of him, there was a red winged blackbird perched on cattails. Their perfect place to relax and think; above was a golden eagle flying over the lake. James lost track of time, he had been there almost three hours. It was time he went home to get some sleep. As much as he hated to leave he looked around one last time before his drive home. When he arrived home he went straight to bed.

At five in the morning his phone rang. It was Craig, with unpleasant news. Someone left a message for Lewis on his doorstep. James put on some jeans and a t-shirt, then raced to his home. He ran inside to find out what was happening, Craig was there.

"Someone left this for him. I don't like this; we have to find this maniac."

It was an ax carved with the words in the handle:

THIS IS YOUR LAST CHANCE, BACK OFF

"James, I'm putting him in protective custody. I'm not willing to risk his life."

"I understand, sir, I agree with you one hundred percent."

"Wait a minute, don't I have a say in all this?"

"I'm sorry, Lewis, but you don't. We've lost too many lives as is and we're not risking yours, regardless of what's at stake. You're in protective custody and that's final."

Lewis pulled James aside and tried to explain that he could help, but he needs to be in his own home. James wouldn't back down. They would think of something else, but not this way. James had something he had to do, then he promised Lewis he would be back to fill him in on anything he could find. Another call came in from the Duncan's. They too had a message left on their doorstep. James asked Craig to take care of Lewis while he went to the Duncan's. When he arrived, Mr. Duncan was at the door. Diane knew nothing about what had happened, and he wanted to keep it that way. They went into his home office and he locked the door.

"This box was on my doorstep when I went for the morning paper."

Another ax with a carved message:

YOU'RE RESPONSIBLE

"What do you think this means? What could I possibly be responsible for?"

"You have to remember; we're dealing with someone who has a very sick mind. Nothing is going to make sense to us, but it all makes sense to this demented mind."

"I don't want Diane to find out about any of this, can you help me?"

"The only way I can help you with that and make sure your protected, is to have you leave town. This time I'm not giving you a choice. A friend of mine is moving here and he just received an ax message. He's in protective custody but he's assisting with this case, the psychological angles. I want you both out of town within the next hour. I don't care where you go, keep in touch, this is my cell number. I'll keep you up to date. I realize this is an inconvenience, but better that than dead."

"I'm sorry, but I can't do that. Why can't you just give us protective custody as well?"

"Men are limited and we want to cover all the grounds."

"Well, we do have a vacation coming up. I suppose now would be as good a time as any."

"Great! You take care of that, and I'll take care of things here. Just call me before you board the plane."

James called Jeff so he wouldn't call the Duncan's and not get an answer and worry about what was happening. Of course he wouldn't tell Rebecca. Jeff heard her calling to him, then told James he would get back to him later.

"Is anything wrong?"

"No, no, really. I have this incredible craving for cheesecake with chocolate syrup and a strawberry shake right now."

"Alright, sounds interesting. There's a diner in town that has great food. I'm sure they can serve you whatever you want."

Jeff drove her into town. They talked on their way. Rebecca looked like she was ready to give birth at any moment.

"Are you sure you should be eating that stuff?"

"It's a craving! Remember, I'm pregnant."

Without saying another word, he drove a little faster. They went in and sat at a table then ordered lunch. They enjoyed the conversation so much, it didn't seem long at all when their food was served. He asked her about what she had hoped for in life. She began thinking about Wes and how they had planned on having children and buying their dream home. Now she could only concentrate on part of that dream.

"Your dreams can still come true, not with Wes, but someone as lovely as you should have no trouble finding someone."

"Maybe, I'm not sure yet. I was in town with your mother the other day and we were in the cutest little store, not far from here. I saw an adorable quilt I would like to pick up for the baby. Would we have time to stop there?"

"I don't see why not. Let me pay the check then we'll leave."

They walked over, looking around. Rebecca seemed to be enjoying herself. Merchandise like this could not be found in any store back in Arizona. As they were checking out, a television nearby flashed a news bulletin about the warnings to the Duncan's and Lewis, she became worried about what was happening. She wanted to talk to James or go back home. That was the choice she gave Jeff. He handed her his cell phone to call James, his only hope was that James would get through to her. He told her not to worry, that they went on vacation shortly after. What he couldn't figure out was how the news reached Iowa. Right now, that didn't matter. He had to put an end to this once and for all. Again he went to talk to Lewis, but he didn't have anything new to add to what they did have already. Paula was getting off work in a few hours and James would be there to follow her home. There was one idea, but James didn't care for it, although he may consider it as a last resort.

He went to the shop as she was getting in her car. He followed her home, then approached her as she was unlocking her door.

"What are you doing here?"

"I need to talk to you, your life may be in danger."

"How do you figure that?"

"The Duncan's, and a friend of mine, both, found an ax on their doorstep this morning. Both had messages carved in the handle. Since all this began with Bill, I don't want you put in jeopardy."

"I still don't see how this involves me. As I recall, all the victims were men, is that correct?"

"Yes, but I'm not taking any chances. Remember what happened to Rebecca?"

"Yes but she's pregnant."

"Her pregnancy may not have anything to do with this"

"As I recall, the note indicated she was carrying a demon child. That was a threat against her baby, not her."

"She is carrying the baby, and if they want the baby gone, she would have to go as well. Now, I'm not taking any chances."

"Well, you're not, but I am, and I said no."

James couldn't believe how bull headed she was. He sat in the living room while she went to change. Suddenly he heard her scream. After he ran in to see what had happened, he saw on her mirror what looked like a message in blood.

YOU WILL DIE

"That's enough, now pack some things and let's go. I'll have a crew in here going over this with a fine tooth comb."

As he was looking around he found a picture of Paula when she was younger, standing with a woman. Looking at the face of the little girl, you could tell it was Paula, and the woman with her could be her mother.

"Who is this?"

"That is my mother. She left a long time ago. I never heard from her again. She left me with my stepfather. I hated him."

"Why did you hate him?"

"He abused me sexually. He died just before I left. No love loss. I never knew how to find my father. My mother never talked about him, or kept any pictures of him. She was very bitter when it came to him. After a while of pumping for information about him, I learned not to ask again. Don't get me wrong, my mother never abused me, she was just very bitter."

"I'm very sorry."

"No need to be, I got over it and learned to move on with my life. That's why I moved her, to forget. Rebecca has been like a sister to me from the time I arrived in town. That's why she's so important to me. She was always there for me."

"I understand. We all have someone like that in our lives. I'm so sorry for what you've been through."

"Please, don't be, like I said, I've moved on with my life. Wait a minute, what's wrong here? We're talking and I never liked you! Now I guess I need you. I never thought I would ever be nice towards you!"

"Yes, well, maybe now you realize I'm on your side. So you better finish up and let's get out of here."

"You sound awfully sure of yourself."

"I'm generally very sure of myself. Comes with the territory."

After she was through packing, he drove her to a seedy hotel the police used as a safe house for victims. The atmosphere was terrible, but if she were safe, she would do her best to put up with this room. She began to try and clean things up as best as she could, but you can only do so much with a place like this. James stepped out of the room briefly, for a few minutes. When he came back, Paula was curious as to what he was doing. He told her he sent one of the policewomen out for a few things. There were shabby drapes on the windows and no phone. He wants to make her stay here as comfortable as possible, if possible.

"What am I supposed to do about my job?"

"Don't worry, I'll have someone take you back and forth. Until this is over, I want to make sure you're protected."

"Protected? I'm going to feel more like a prisoner. Is this really necessary?"

"It is, if you want to stay alive."

"Can't I just be protected in my own apartment?"

"I want you out of the equation. We're still not sure what exactly we're dealing with, and I'm not risking anyone's life. The killer was in your apartment; doesn't that make you feel invaded?"

"Well, of course it does, you think I like strangers helping themselves to my personal life, people I don't even know?"

"All right, then this is necessary."

"I'm sorry, I'm on edge. I miss my best friend, and being here is no help. I mean…well, you know what I mean."

"Yes, I do, and I wish things could be different. All I can say is they will be when this is all over. I can't do more than that. I wish I could, but I can't."

"I realize that, and I'm sorry for being such a pain. Have you heard from Rebecca?"

"I know she's fine. She's away from all this madness, that has to be a plus. Look I know how this must feel, but believe me, I want this to end as much as you do. Once this is over, you can get back to your normal life. Officer

Grayson will be back soon. I have things to do, but I will be back later. Hang in there."

Paula looked out the window as James left. She watched him get in his car and pull out his cell phone. She couldn't help but wonder what he was up to, and to whom he was talking. As soon as he left and was outside in his car, he called Jeff to check on them. They were fine and he let them know everything was fine here, with the exception of what happened to Paula, but he rather Rebecca didn't know anything about that. The Duncan's were fine. No more threats or attempts with them, but he promised to keep in touch. When they finished their conversation, Jeff went inside into the kitchen. When he did, he laughed so hard he thought he would burst.

"What is so funny? You would think this is the first time you ever saw me baking?"

"Not you, but, I'm sorry, I can't help myself. Rebecca just looks like a ghost with flour covering her face."

"Alright, Mr. Funny pants, let's see you have a crack at this. I'm just teaching her a few things, and when you're learning, you're bound to have a bit of a mess. Once she gets the hang of it, she'll be a pro like me."

"I'm sorry I don't mean to make fun. I just couldn't help myself."

"Oh, I'm sure you couldn't. I only hope I can someday be as good at this as your mother. Right now I have my doubts."

"Don't worry, you'll be fine. If you only knew how mom was at this when she first started baking."

"Oh really, and just how would you know about that?"

"Dad, of course."

"Tonight there's a dance in town. Maybe Rebecca would like to go."

"Oh I don't know, I'm not a very good dancer."

"Jeff is; he'll have you dancing in no time. You'll have a great time."

"That's a great idea! I promise you will have the best time. As far as dancing, I won first prize in a contest in my younger days. There's nothing to it, you'll be a pro by the end of the evening."

Jeff wanted to talk to his mother in private, to update her on some information. They were talking for a few minutes when they heard a cry, then a crash in the kitchen; they rushed in and found a broken glass on the floor, along with Rebecca unconscious. They rushed over to help her. Jeff carried her into the living room, laying her on the sofa. His mother came in with some smelling salts, but by then, she was beginning to come around.

"What happened?"

"I don't know. I was getting some water when I felt a little dizzy. I remember dropping a glass; oh, I'm so very sorry, Mrs. Fanala."

"That's perfectly alright, don't worry about it, as long as you're alright."

"I'm sorry, I suppose I've had too much excitement. I think I'd like to go lay down awhile, if you don't mind."

"Not at all, now you go rest up for tonight."

"Mom, what do you suppose happened?"

"She's pregnant dear, things like this happen. You worry too much, she'll be fine. I should know, I already went through this."

Rebecca went to rest, but Jeff was very concerned. His mother reassured him everything was fine, reminding him that she is pregnant and will have times like this.

"She looks as though she is due soon. How many more months does she have?"

"I believe it's another month and a half. She wants to have here baby in Arizona. I only hope it will work out for her like that. She's had too many disappointments already. It's very important to her."

"Well, if comes to the point where that may not happen, would it be so bad if she had her baby here?"

"No, of course not. She feels that way about it, but she would really like to be back home. I can understand that. Well, I have some things in town I have to attend to, so let me give you a hand in the kitchen before I leave."

Jeff went back to the kitchen to help his mother clean up, then went for a drive into town. He was still here on business, even though it felt as though he were on vacation. He was in town for two hours, and then he stopped to pick up a corsage for Rebecca before heading back home. She's a beautiful woman and starting to get to him. He had to be strong; after all, she is his client, for now. Jeff drove a little slower on the way back. He had forgotten just how beautiful his hometown is and he did enjoy being back. There was a lot for him to think about and he just couldn't shake anything. Especially after the last phone call from James. The information he gave him was pretty remarkable, but for now, he tried to concentrate more on Rebecca and leave the rest to James. When he arrived back at the house, his mother filled him in on what was happening. She could hear sounds from Rebecca's room as though she were crying, but didn't want to impose on her. He couldn't stand the thought of her hurting and went into the room where she was resting, and knocked on the door.

"Come in."

"Hi! Are you awake?"

"Yes, I am, I just couldn't rest very well."

"I'm sorry. Anything I can help you with?"

"Not real, but thank you."

She sat on the edge of the bed, turned away from him. He walked over, sitting next to her, holding her hand for comfort.

"You know, I'm a very good listener. Talk to me, maybe I can help."

"I really don't think you can, but thank you anyway."

"Alright, let's say I can't, you can still talk to me."

Thinking for a moment, she then took a deep breath. She felt a bit terrible laying her problems on him, but he did offer, and she needed someone to talk to and maybe he could help sort things out.

"All my life, even when I was just a little girl, I dreamed about what my life would be like. I dreamed of a family and home, and spending my days with my husband. Funny how life seems to love curve balls."

"I know. I can't bring back Wes, but I'm a firm believer in everything happening for a reason. We will never know the reason why Wes was taken, but you're going to have his baby; you'll have a small part of him with you always in this child. There's a plan for all of us and we can't control the, but whatever you do, don't give up. Soon you'll have a little human who will depend on you. You can't give up now."

"I realize there are so many people who love me and want to help but even if you put all them in one room, I would still feel alone."

"Someday you'll find someone again, and he won't be like Wes, but you'll both be in love, a different love than the kind you had with Wes. I didn't know him, but don't you think he would want it that way?"

"You're right, he would. Well, look at the time, I should be getting ready if we're going tonight. Are you sure you want to risk my breaking your foot?" "I'm sure you're not that bad. I'd better get ready myself. I hope I was some kind of help to you. At least you're not bottling it up inside. See you soon."

Jeff went in the kitchen and sat with his mother to talk. He told her as much as he could, without betraying

James trust. What a horrid thing for anyone to have to live through. Rebecca is a very lovely young woman and shouldn't have to suffer like this, but things have a way of working out, and they will for her as well.

"She's too wonderful not to have a happy life and share it with someone who loves her. It will happen for her someday. Enough of the darkness you better get ready for the dance. I'll check on Rebecca and see if she needs anything. You run along and get dressed."

"I've really missed being here, but I do love the city. I may have a surprise for you before we leave. It has everything to do with my business here."

"Well, I hope it's a pleasant one. We've had enough doom and gloom for a long time."

"I'm sure it will be."

He saw the expression on her face and how happy she's been since he arrived.

"Mom! I love you."

"I love you, too, now go get ready for the dance."

He went to get ready for the evening. Walking in his room, he made a phone call to James; he just had to talk to him. There wasn't much more he had to tell Jeff, other than it could all be over with soon. James was sitting in his office when O'Leary brought him a package that had been delivered. Someone somehow dropped it off, no one knows who. The card taped to the package had James name stenciled on the envelope. Inside there was a card and all it read was:

YOU'RE RUNNING SHORT OF TIME

James began to open the package, but then he heard it ticking. He ordered O'Leary to get everyone out of the building and called for the bomb squad to take care of the package. Two members of the squad arrived, carefully opening the package. When they did, it turned out it was just a clock with a note.

THIS TIME YOU'RE LUCKY, NEXT TIME YOU MAY NOT BE.

"A hoax, it was only a hoax. Take this to forensics and call everyone back. I want a report ASAP! Make sure they know that."

"Yes sir, right away."

The phone rang and all he heard was laughing on the other end. It sounded like one of those laughing boxes you buy at a joke store. He slammed the receiver down as anger tore through him like wildfire. What a sick sense of humor anyone could have. Next, his cell phone rang.

"Who the hell is this?"

"James? This is Lewis, are you alright?"

"I'm sorry, I'm fine. What's up?"

He needed James to rush over. Lewis had a visitor and he wanted James to see for himself what was happening. This was getting to close to home; James rushed over in his car with the lights on to clear the way. James wanted him bad, now more than ever. When he arrived he walked up to the door and found a note attached to an ax and stained with fake blood, the kind kids use for Halloween. The note read;

THIS IS YOUR FINAL WARNING, BACK OFF

James filled him in on the package that was delivered and the phone call he received shortly after. If whoever this sick person is, and if he's trying to tick him off, it's working.

"Have you thought about what I told you?"

"Yes I have, but there is no possible way it could be, not a chance."

They sat down to discuss things a little more, but James needed proof, somehow. Yet, he wouldn't dismiss the idea all together. They sat and talked most of the night when Lewis came up with an idea, but James thought it was ludicrous, but was willing to give it a try. The next morning, James stopped to pick up Paula and drive her to work, even though she wasn't in the best of spirits. She explained she couldn't sleep very well in those surroundings. He understood how she felt, but it had to be this way. Paula wanted to take her mind off of things and began talking about a baby shower for Rebecca. She was due soon to deliver her baby, and hopefully be back home when she did give birth. She wanted to contact Wes's family to see if they could make it in. That would be a wonderful surprise for Rebecca. They talked for a while before he parked in front of the shop where she worked.

"Don't forge, I'll pick you up after work, so do not leave without me."

"Yes sir, I will be here. Thank you very much."

"I'm not kidding."

"I understand and I will be here! Get a grip. See you later."

Paula steps out of the car, promising she will wait for him, but only if he will take her to dinner and maybe a bit of shopping. Being locked up in that room was more than she could take. She wanted to pick up some things to help make her stay a little more bearable. She went inside the shop and found Mr. Langdon waiting for her.

"Good morning, I hope you're feeling better."

"Much better, thank you."

"Paula, I need a favor. I'm waiting for an important phone call, but I have to get this money in the bank. Would you mind going for me, please? Mr. Duncan knows you, besides, I already called him to tell him you will be making the deposit this time."

"Sure, no problem, I'd be happy to make the deposit."

The bank wasn't far and the walk was pleasant, but she still missed having

Rebecca around. It seems like she's been gone for months, instead of a couple of weeks. On her way to the bank, she passed a baby store, so she stopped to look through the window. There are so many things in this store that Rebecca can use. During lunch, she made plans as to whom she was going to invite, the menu and more. For now, she had to make the bank deposit. The bank was almost empty, excluding the tellers. From a distance, she saw Mr. Duncan and rushed over to try and get some information about Rebecca.

"Mr. Duncan!"

"Paula, it's good to see you. How have you been?"

"I'm fine, thank you. I'm planning a baby shower for Rebecca and was wondering if you could tell me when she'll be back."

"I wish I could, but really, I have no idea. All she told me was she needed to get away for a while. Of course I understood, so I told her to take all the time she needed. She did say she would call me when she's ready. I can contact you when she does, if that would help?"

"Yes it would. Thank you so much, I appreciate that."

"I'd love to chat awhile, but I really have a lot to do today. It was nice seeing you again. Take care of yourself."

Paula rushed back to the shop, excited about the shower, but a little frustrated. After a few minutes, she decided it really was for her own good. When she walked in through the door, she found Mr. Langdon still waiting for his phone call. The day was busy and went by fairly quickly. People were shopping for birthdays, weddings, anniversaries; this time of year was always busy for them. When the day was over, Paula collected her things and waited outside for James. As he promised, he bought her dinner and was planning on shopping afterwards. She had her mouth set on Chinese, so they went to the nearest place they could find. The restaurant was small and quaint; the decorations made the customers feel as though they were in China. They talked during dinner and James was beginning to grow on Paula, but she still was cautious.

He told her about the box and the phone call he received at the office. He also told her about the note attached to Lewis's door. Immediately, the color drained from her face and her hands began to shake.

Paula! Paula, what's wrong?"

He touched her shoulder as she turned to look at him.

"He's going to kill again isn't he?"

"Not if I can help it. Try and calm down."

James dropped some money on the table then held her arm and led her out the door as quickly as he could. The air would do her some good. He walked her around for a couple of blocks, until she was able to get a hold of herself.

"He's going to kill again, isn't he?"

"I won't lie to you, that is a possibility, but why did you get so shaken up?"

"When you told me about the ax, I had a vision of what Bill must have looked like with an ax in his chest. You've got to find him before…"

"O, Paula, calm down, calm down. I will find him, and when I do, everyone will be safe again. I promise you that."

"I would really like to leave now. Please take me home."

"Paula!"

"Please take me home."

She moved so quickly, James practically had to run just to keep up with her. He unlocked the car door and she jumped in, shutting the door and not giving him a chance. Her head was in her hand as if something were wrong.

"Are you going to be alright?"

"Yes, I'll be fine. Let's just please go back to the motel."

James drove until they were back. Even that place was great to see. Once she was inside she sat in the chair with her eyes closed.

"Paula, is there anything I can get you?"

"A couple of aspirin would be great. I'm getting a headache."

While he was in the bathroom getting the aspirin, he heard her scream. As he rushed out, he was hit on the back of his head and left unconscious. With his hands tied behind his back and duct tape on his mouth, he was left locked in the bathroom. While unconscious, everything was going through his head from the beginning of this case, up until present. Each murder case went through his head including the morgue when he took Rebecca, all the notes. The more that went through his head, the more he worked his way back to a conscience state. When he finally did, he struggled a short time to get his hands free. After twenty minutes, he was free, removed the tape from his face, then kicked the door in to get to Paula. She was handcuffed to the bed with a blindfold and tape over her mouth. Her face had a red mark on her cheek as though she were slapped, and hard. When he un cuffed her and removed the tape from her face, she began screaming.

"Please don't hurt me, please. I'm begging you."

"Paula, it's me, James."

He removed her blindfold. She was so happy to see him, she sat up and nearly choked him with her arms around his neck. Gently, he pulled her arms away to look at her.

"Are you alright, you're shaking terribly?"

"I am now. I was laying here when I heard a movement. When I turned to look, there was someone standing there with a black ski mask on. I screamed and that was when he hit me and tied me up. He was headed towards the bathroom, but I couldn't warn you because he threatened me with a gun. I'm so sorry."

Paula burst into tears. She was so very shaken. How did he get past the officers on duty? The one outside the door was hit so hard on his head, James had called the ambulance in case he had a concussion. When he checked with the others, they all swore no one got past them. He ordered them to send the ambulance attendants to Paula's room, where one of the men was injured, then he went back to Paula.

"I want out of here, I can't stay here another minute. I'd feel safer in my own apartment."

As much as he hated to admit, she was probably right. She gathered her things as quickly as possible and was gone in no time. Paula was still a bit hysterical and had every right to be, but James did what he could to calm her. When he pulled up in front of her building, she couldn't get out of the car fast enough and practically ran to the door, only to find an ax with a note.

YOU MUST DIE, DEVIL

When she turned to run, James was behind her and caught her looking at the ax in the door. This is still not a safe place for her to stay. There was another alternative, the Duncan's. Right away he called the Duncan's, as he escorted Paula back to his car. They had no problem taking her in. Diane enjoyed her stay the first time. He would take her over as soon as someone arrived to handle what happened at Paula's. He no sooner dropped her off and was leaving when his phone rang; it was Jeff. He was calling because Rebecca felt like something was wrong and wouldn't rest until she knew for sure. James found it fascinating. It was almost like a sixth sense type of thing. He told Jeff everything that transpired that evening. Of course, Jeff couldn't tell Rebecca that. Then again, he didn't want to have to lie to her. Instead, he just told her everything was fine. They were now, but he left out everything that had happened prior to what happened. After all, she was about ready to have a baby; it was for her own good;

Jeff said he would keep in touch, but for now he had to go. Rebecca was waiting to go for a walk. It seemed to relax her and helped her to sleep. They seemed to enjoy each other's company a little more. Jeff did whatever he could to satisfy her needs. They walked around for about an hour and he told her everything was fine back home. Except, Paula was missing her, so Diane invited her to stay with them until she flew back home.

"How does ice cream sound? My mother makes the best blueberry ice cream you ever tasted."

"That sounds really good right now. I never had homemade ice cream."

"Once you had it, you'll never want store bought again. It's not difficult making homemade ice cream, just a little time."

"Then I'd love some, maybe it'll cool us off."

They walked back to the house and not only did she make the ice cream, but blueberry pie to go with it. They all had a large serving and sat on the porch talking about most anything. Including when Jeff was a small child.

"Don't need to hear this. I've lived it, so if you'll all excuse me, I have something I need to do."

Once again, he called James to let him know that Rebecca has been talking about coming home. As much as she was enjoying herself, she really wanted her baby to be born back in Arizona. James talked him into trying to convince her to stay a little bit longer. He believed he was close to finding the murderer. If not, she could come home, but under protection. Right now he had to leave, he was in the middle of planning something big. Lewis was in his office and they were making plans together. He was so sure his suspicions were correct. It took a lot of convincing to sell James on his idea. Lewis didn't have a shred of evidence, but everything he told James, no matter how crazy, everything he told him so far seemed to follow through. James wanted him so bad he was willing to try anything. They sat in his office all night, going over files and planning until every detail was perfect. They would only have one shot at this, so it had to be perfect.

The next day, Brad drove Paula to work. She seemed exhausted after the evening she put in, but insisted she would be just fine.

"I will pick you up after work, then we're going to meet Diane at the steakhouse. Do you think you'll feel up to it? If not, we can do this another night."

"Oh no, I'll be fine. I don't want to spoil anyone's evening. I'll be fine after I have some coffee in me. I'll see you after work."

Hopefully she would be able to keep busy today. All she had was the trust she put in James to handle all of this. From what he was saying, he might have had a plan he was sure would work. It would be great if all this could be over with, and her best friend could come back home again. The passing months have seemed like a lifetime. Brad was on his way to the bank. He was sitting at a red light when it turned green and he began to proceed. He was struck by a speeding car. His car spun, then slammed into a light pole. When the air bags burst open, he was blinded momentarily. When he could see, he stepped out of his car for some air. He was a little shaky, but he leaned on the car, coughing from the smoke after the air bags opened. The fire trucks and police were nearby and were on the scene instantly. The police asked him to sit in his car until the ambulance arrived. The police were taking statements when the ambulance attendants arrived; they rushed over to check out Brad. They told him it would be best if he went to the hospital to be examined, to play it safe, and asked him if they could call anyone for him.

James was at the station and received word about what had happened. When they told him it was a female who struck him, he was assured it was not who he was looking for, but still wanted to know how Brad was. He told the officer on duty he would pick up Brad's wife and meet them at the hospital. James called her to let her know he was on his way to pick her up, but it took a lot of convincing that it had nothing to do with this case. He stayed with her at the hospital until Brad was released, then drove them both home. After he made sure they were all right he went to the shop to let Paula know what had happened and that he would be the one picking her up after work.

"This is crazy! I don't need a sitter in broad daylight. I can take a bus."

"Or I can take you home, if it's alright with the officer."

"Mr. Langdon, I can't impose on you like that."

"What impose, I'm offering. So it's settled, I'll take you home."

"Thank you, Mr. Langdon, I'd appreciate this very much. As for you, young lady, listen to your boss. I'll talk to you later."

"Wait! Are you absolutely sure one has nothing to do with the other?"

"I promise you it doesn't. I'll see you later."

James went back to the station to look over some information Lewis had given him. He read files and journals and still the whole thing seemed a bit outlandish. After tonight, he would see just how outlandish it all really is, that's if everything went as planned. This is a tremendous risk, but he had no choice but to go through with this. Time had passed, it was after six already. He wanted to check on Paula before anything. When he called the Duncan residence, Paula answered almost before the phone rang.

"That was fast, it's as if you knew I was calling."

"That's ridiculous, I've been waiting all day to talk to you. Have you found out anything yet?"

"Nothing yet, but hopefully by tomorrow at this time we all will go back to our normal lives again."

They talked for half an hour before Paula said she had a terrible headache and just wanted to go to bed early. She was pleased to hear that if all went well, Rebecca would be coming back home. That was the best news, now she can plan her shower. For now, she just wanted some relief from her headache.

"Take care of your headache. We'll talk again."

James left his office to visit with Lewis for a while, about two hours. All that was left was to wait. Lewis was going over some notes from the patients he had today. He made notes on his tape recorder and listened to some sessions he had taped, normal procedure for him. For a short, time he had stopped to take a break. He went into the kitchen to make some coffee. He looked at the clock on the wall, it was nearly ten thirty. Turned out to be a quiet evening, so he went to bed. When he walked into his bedroom, there was an ax with a note attached planted in his bed.

CONTINUE AND YOU WILL DIE

Immediately he called James. He said he would be right there. Lewis looked around for a broken window or unlocked door, which couldn't be possible, he had James lock everything before he left. How did anyone get in without him hearing a sound? Lewis heard the sirens and went downstairs to meet James. He showed the police to his bedroom. James went over and saw the note.

"How did he get in? Are you sure you didn't hear anything?"

"I'm positive. Listen, I'm just as angry as you. You don't think I want this to end?"

"You're right, I'm sorry. The last thing we should do is attack each other, we have to work together on this."

James had the police go over every inch of the house and had O'Leary take the ax and note to the station. First priority, as usual. He never liked being beat, and this deranged person won't beat him either. Obviously they were getting close, or this wouldn't be happening right now.

"My men will be here awhile; I have to check the Duncan home. I will be right back."

He rushed over, pounding on their door when he arrived. Brad answered and James burst in through the door.

"I need to know everyone is here and accounted for. Where are the girls?"

"Brad! What's going on?"

"I'm sorry, Mrs. Duncan, to bother you so late, but I need to know everyone here is alright."

"Well, as you can see, we're fine. What is this?"

"Where is Paula?"

"In her room, sleeping of course. I gave her a sleeping pill to help her sleep. She had such a headache and she had difficulty sleeping."

James ran up the stairs as fast as he could, then into Paula's room. He turned on the light and she rustled a bit. When she rolled over and opened her eyes, she saw him standing there.

"What's wrong?"

"I just had to be sure you're alright. I'm sorry, go back to sleep. How is your headache?"

"Actually, I forgot all about it. Diane gave me a sleeping pill and it worked so well, my headache is gone."

"Good. I'm glad. I'll see you in the morning."

He turned out the light and closed the door behind him.

"I'm sorry to have disturbed you."

"Well at least you're doing your job, whatever that is for tonight. Goodnight, Mr. Garrett."

"Don't worry about her, she is always a bit testy when she misses her sleep."

"I understand. Again, please accept my apologies."

Something had to give, this couldn't continue like this. He stopped back at the station for some information, not really expecting anything new, before he went home. There was something different, some blood found on the ax. Not fake blood, but real blood, A positive. It wasn't much, but it was something to work with. Now all he needed was the killer, but who's to say his blood is A positive. He went home with the results and thought he would call Lewis in the morning. His adrenaline was pumping and he couldn't sleep. He couldn't help but feel he was getting even closer to closing this case. It was almost two A.M. when his phone rang. When he answered, again there was that mechanical laugh on the other end. This was turning into a game; one he didn't care for. This time, there was part of a child's poem recited by a voice, possibly from the television.

"You can't catch me."

"Whoever this is, I will catch you."

Again, the laugh came online then a click followed. This time he couldn't wait for morning; he immediately called Lewis. He remembered something and promised to get back to James in the morning. Since this case began, it's been nothing but long days and nights. Hopefully his plan would bring it to an end.

CHAPTER 6

In Iowa, the Fanala's were planning on celebrating their wedding anniversary. They've been together for thirty years. Jeff was ready to leave when Rebecca caught him.

"Where are you off to this early?"

"For a walk, want to join me?"

"I'd love to; I didn't know you liked to walk so much."

He held the door and with his hand on the small of her back, guided her out to the porch. Jeff explained about it being his parents wedding anniversary and wanted to pick out something, but he didn't know what to get. She had offered to go with him to help, if he wouldn't mind her tagging along. The way he felt, he was glad to have her along.

"So what do you think?"

"How many years will it be?"

"Thirty years."

"Hmmm, thirty. That's the pearl and diamond year."

His mother would be easy, but his father would be a bit more difficult. Then again, maybe not.

"I have it, how about a pearl necklace for your mother and a diamond chip watch for your father? I was thinking a diamond chip right at twelve. I thought he might wear that instead of the face trimmed in diamonds."

"You're right, that would be perfect. I knew there was a reason for you to take this trip with me."

"Please, I'm sure you would have thought of something."

They stopped at the jewelers and Rebecca helped him find the perfect watch and necklace. He told the jeweler to wrap it and he would be by later to pick it up, he still had errands to run. Next was the cake, they stopped at the bakery and picked out a red velvet cake with whipped cream icing. His mother's favorite.

"You know; my mother thinks a great deal about you. You're a very likeable person. My father loves you, too. It's great of you to help me like this."

"Well, I don't mind, and I'm very fond of your parents."

"Look at the time, we didn't have breakfast yet. How about we stop and grab a bite before we go back?"

"I'd love to, thank you."

This felt so great, being part of something so special. They had talked over breakfast about what his business plans were and why he was here. He wanted to surprise his parents, but he plans on opening an office nearby. After breakfast, they went over to the building where he would open his second office. She was very impressed. Jeff had to have been doing very well in his practice. The decorators were hard at work to finish in time for this evening. He was hoping to show the place to his parents as an added surprise.

"I think it's wonderful, it's you. Very professional yet it holds a comfortable atmosphere. Not stuffy."

"Great, that's what I was going for."

"Your parents must be so proud of you."

"They are; they would like it even more if I were near them. I will be more often, but I still enjoy Arizona."

His cell phone rang, when he checked it was James.

"I'm sorry, I have to take this outside. Make yourself at home, let me know if the furniture is comfortable."

James filled him in on what was happening. Not even Jeff could believe what he was saying. He told Jeff this could all be over soon then he could bring Rebecca back home.

"She'll be glad to get back. She looks like she could have this baby anytime now, so whatever you have to do, please hurry."

When he walked in his office, she was relaxing in his chair behind his desk. Apparently the furniture was comfortable. Without giving any of the details, he told her they could be going back home soon. She was thrilled, but for now wanted to concentrate on the Anniversary. They went back to pick up the gifts and the cake, then drove back to the ranch. Rebecca wanted to do the cooking and planned something special. She promised the celebration would be a great one. Together they planned how they would surprise his parents. She told him what her thoughts would be and he gave her the money to shop, he had some work to at his office. Afterwards, they would meet for lunch and drive back to the house. As soon as she left, Jeff called James for an update of what was happening back home. James explained he had a plan, but it didn't pan out so they would need more time. They were going to try again, but it was imperative that he keep Rebecca in Iowa, for now. Jeff told him how anxious she is to get back home.

"I understand this must be difficult and how she must want to come back, but we are closer to ending this than you know. I'll tell you what, if we don't have this wrapped up by the end of the week, you can bring her home, but just give me four days, that's all I need."

"I'm sure I can manage that. However, if worse comes to worse, there must be a way to protect her at home?"

"There's more involved than just protection, and I don't have time to get into that right now, but believe me, it is for her own good. At least for now."

"There's more to this than you're telling me, isn't there?"

"Yes there is, but I can't get into the details. You'll just have to trust me and keep Rebecca there."

"Alright, if it's that bad, I'm sure I can manage. Is there anything I can do to help?"

"You're doing it by keeping her there. I'll be in touch."

The Ax

James was with Lewis at his home, going over the plans to put an end to this nightmare and regain the peace this town once had.

"We'll have to wait until this evening before we can put this in motion, but trust me, I know this better than you realize. Lives are at stake and I wouldn't steer you wrong about something so important."

"I do trust you, it's just pretty incredible information. I've read about things like this, but I have never been so up close and personally involved in the real thing before. So, good luck and let the games begin."

They went over the plans at least half a dozen times, until they were both convinced this would work. Lewis had cancelled his appointments for the day so he could help James, and maybe even get caught up on some paper work. James left, promising to be nearby if Lewis would need him. After Lewis showed him to the door, he went into his home office to get started. The atmosphere was erratic, but how else could it be, considering what could happen if there was even one mistake. The house was silent, except for the clocks ticking. Time was passing slowly, giving Lewis an uneasy feeling and making it difficult to get anything done, maybe too quiet. Coffee sounded good right about now, and there was some biscotti one of his patients made for him, that would top off the coffee. Lewis tried to talk his way out of the spooky feelings he was having, waiting for the excitement to happen, but no matter where in the house he went, the silence was intense.

He sat at the table with his coffee, and thoughts pouring through his head. After about thirty minutes he went back to his office. Just as he walked through the door, the clock struck nine. It was time to begin. As he walked over to his desk, opened the drawer and pulled out a slip of paper with a phone number scribbled on it. He picked up the phone and dialed the number, then waited for someone to answer. After the fourth ring, he heard a voice say hello on the other end.

"Hello, Paul! It's been a long time. I just moved into town, why don't you stop over and see me?"

He quickly rattled off his address when Paul became extremely upset and wanted to know how he got his number.

"Paul, calm down, remember your temper. I'm new in town and thought we could get together. I saw you once, so I thought I'd call you and we could get together, that's all."

Lewis sat there listening to Paul screaming at him and trying to intercede, but failed. It was obvious he made him very angry, and the angrier he became, the better the chance of his plan working. Finally, he heard a click, then a dial tone. Again, Lewis dials the phone, but this time it's James.

"Everything is set."

That was all he really needed to say before he hung up. What was left now is to wait. Wait, hope, and pray that the plan would go as smoothly as it did when he and James discussed the details the night before. Now if he could only hang on to his self-confidence and courage, then he would be well prepared for anything that could happen. Time seemed to move even slower still, and more intense. He walked to the window, looking up at the big bright moon in the sky, shining down and filling the street with light.

Even the night was uneasy. There was a bang in the living room. He took a deep breath then went to check it out. Slowly, he walked in, looking all around for anyone who may have been in the house. He walked towards the living room slowly. Once he was in the room, he noticed the shutters banging. A wind was stirring up; the trees were swaying back and forth. As much as he wanted the culprit caught, he wanted this all to be over with. When he turned, there was Paul standing in the living room doorway.

"Hello Paul. It's been a long time. I heard you were back. What happened?"

Paul tilted his head slightly as if he didn't understand what he meant by that question. A little at a time he walked into the room, sideways, not towards Lewis, and never taking his eyes off him, even for a second. Anticipation filled the room, that and tension.

"I see you still have a fetish for the ax. I thought we took care of that during our meetings years ago."

Paul spoke with a frog type voice, as if he had problems with his throat.

"Is that why you brought me here, to talk about the ax?"

'Not exactly, but you didn't answer my question. I thought you gave them up?"

"You would like it if I gave them up, wouldn't you? Well, this ax has your name on it. For a long time, I saved this one just for you."

The tension grew thicker as Lewis tried not to show how nervous he was.

"I see. What have I ever done to you Paul? I only tried to help you."

"NO! You were supposed to help my sister, but you failed her."

"How did I fail her?"

"She trusted you, and instead, you made her feel as though what happened to her was her fault."

"I never meant to make her feel that way, those were not my intensions."

"However, you did. What happened to her was not her fault. You act as though she enjoyed it, like it was fun for her. That's not how it was. You made her feel dirty. You ruined her."

Clearly, he was becoming angrier the more he tried to talk to him.

"Paul, that was not my plan. In fact, I thought she was showing improvement, until she stopped coming in for her sessions."

"I told her to stop, you weren't helping her. Instead, she digressed."

"You have to understand, depression is a terrible thing and it does happen, but if she wouldn't have stopped, I could have helped her. She was improving. I believe I was helping her."

"LIAR"

Paul picked up a vase and smashed it on the floor.

"You believe? Do you also believe you're God? Do you believe you hold that much power, that you can heal anyone, anytime you want?"

"That's not what I'm saying, no one can do that, but I could have helped her. I still can. I've had patients just like your sister and I have helped them. I'd like another chance, but I need to talk to your sister."

"My sister despises you, she doesn't want to see you."

"If you talk to her, she will listen to you. Convince her to come back I can help her."

"Why would I do that, so you can strip her of her sanity?"

Again, he chose another item to break, but this time threw it against the wall near Lewis. The more he tried to talk to him, the angrier he became. Soon, there was no use trying.

"You know that isn't true. I want to help her, help her live a happy normal life again."

"I'll tell you what I do know, I know it's time for you to die."

"Listen to me, I need to talk to Paula."

"You will never talk to her as long as I have anything to say about it, so quit stalling, shrink. Your time has come."

Lewis picked up a poker next to the fireplace, ready to defend himself.

"Do you really think you can defeat me?"

"I'd rather try to help you. I don't want to hurt you, or Paula."

"You dare to stand there and lie to me as you did to her."

"I'm not telling you lies; I want to help."

"You're trying to defend all the monsters, like dear old step daddy. They are the ones who need to be stopped. I'm doing the world a justice by ridding them of such attackers."

"Attackers is a strange word for you to use. Don't you consider yourself an attacker? Think about what you've done to those innocent men."

"They were abusers of a different kind. An abuser, is an abuser no matter how."

"Again, we're back to you and your attacks."

"Enough of this game, your time has come, NOW!"

"Paul, please listen to me, I want to help."

"You don't know how to help anyone, and now you can't even help yourself."

"Give me a chance to prove to you that I'm right. I will not fail you, but it will not happen overnight."

"That's right, beg for your life as my sister did. It will do you no good."

Paul walked around the room until his back was facing the window. He raised the ax ready to attack Lewis when the sound of glass shattering filled the room. Paul was still standing, with the ax slowly lowering and his eyes as wide as they could be, then he fell to the floor. Lewis stood there a moment, wondering what happened, when James came bursting through the door. Lewis sat in a chair as James walked over to check the body on the floor. Paul spoke a few words to James.

"You don't know what you've done."

Then he looked up at Lewis to tell him it was over, Paul is gone.

"So, I suppose this is when we discover if your theory was correct."

James hesitated a moment, then took a deep breath. As quickly as he could, he removed the ski mask from Paul. He stood up, staring at the body in great disbelief. James didn't know what to say.

"I can't believe the ax murderer was Paula Lived!"

"You can believe it; she was a patient of mine at one time."

"With her disguise, she looked very much like a man."

"A long time ago, she was a patient of mine. Her mother left her second husband because he would beat her. Finally, she had enough and she left, leaving Paula behind. For three years, her stepfather sexually abused her. One day, she snapped. I should say her personality split and she became Paul. As Paul, she killed her stepfather in retaliation with an ax, then she passed out. When she regained conscientiousness, she didn't know what happened, she just called for help and the neighbors called the police."

"This is a horror story. Why would her mother leave her like that?"

"Well, four years later, her mother was found beaten to death. She was mugged on a street corner next to a mailbox. I can only guess that she had just mailed this letter. Her husband threatened to kill them both if she didn't leave by herself and would kill Paula if the police were contacted. She was scared. Her plans were to return and call the police to get Paula back, but she was killed before she could come home."

"No wonder she had two sides to her, after all she went through. Did Paula ever know about her mother wanting to come back for her?"

"No, she didn't. I had hoped that someday I could show her this letter, but it's too late now. My professional opinion is that whenever she felt threatened by a man, or any of her close loved ones, she became Paul and…well you know the rest."

"I've heard and read about situations like this, I see now they were not exaggerated. Paula never stood a chance, did she?"

"Not true, she was showing great improvement, but stopped the sessions. Of course she digressed. I'll never know why she gave up. As Paul just stated a few minutes ago, she told him I made her feel dirty. I think at some point she misunderstood something that was said in one of our meetings, but now I'll never know."

They looked down at the body. James felt the shoulder, realizing she was wearing shoulder pads. The kind football players wear when they're playing a game. When he saw the boots, he removed one; pretty heavy for a boot. Then he realized there was something inside, it was a weight to make the footprint heavier! She had on gloves, but under those gloves were surgical rubber gloves. Everything was so much clearer now, not what he imagined, but at least it's over. Lewis explained that as Paula, she would never think of being so thorough, but as Paul, she was devious. It was part of the split personality she had taken on.

"See, she had this all inside her, but the evil part is the part that she never would have known if it hadn't been for the attacks from her stepfather. Take a look at these journals, particularly the inside cover. Read the inscription."

James opened the journals and was stunned at the inscription.

PAUL DEVIL

"That is her other side, notice the last name is her name spelled backwards. These journals are like trophies. Take them and read them. Inside is how she killed each victim. These are her victories, or rather Paul's victories."

Chills went down his spine; it's like a gory horror movie. The coroner arrived to pick up the body. James began thinking about Rebecca and how she would handle all of this, and in her condition. He told Lewis about her pregnancy and wondered if she would be able to handle this.

"Lewis, I can't thank you enough for all your help, now I have to think about how her best friend is going to handle all this. I don't suppose you could help me with that?"

"Actually, I'd be happy to, call me when you're ready. I'll be there."

"Thank you. I have a call to make; I'll see you tomorrow. Will you be alright?"

"I'll be fine, talk to you later."

James called Jeff to let him know it was over but he would go into details when he came back. He wanted to meet with him, Rebecca, and Lewis to explain some very bad news, and not to mention anything to Rebecca until they could all be together. It was important to her condition that he did not tell her. Jeff, his parents, and Rebecca were outside on the porch playing poker.

"Well mom and dad, I'm afraid I have some business to attend to back in Arizona. I'm afraid Rebecca and I will be flying back tomorrow afternoon. I already reserved our seats on the plane."

"I'm glad. Not that I didn't enjoy myself here, I had a wonderful time, and I can't thank either of you enough for letting me stay here with all of you."

"It was our pleasure. We want to thank you for the lovely party. You really shouldn't have gone to the trouble."

"No trouble. I enjoyed it every bit as much as both of you. It was the least I could do after you invited me into your home, and besides, I really wanted to do that for you. As much as I enjoyed being here, I'm looking forward to being in my own home, I miss my friends and as much as I enjoyed being here, I'm looking forward to being in my own home, not to mention I miss my best friend."

"We hope to see you again. You're welcome here anytime. I suppose we'll be seeing more of you, Jeff, since you're opening an office in town. That was the best anniversary present we ever received."

"Then you'll be happy to know that once I finish in Arizona, I'll be back again to get things started back here. Right now, I better go pack. I'll see all of you in the morning."

"That's a good idea, I think I'll pack my things too. Thank you both again for everything, and I look forward to seeing you again."

His parents talked about what a great time they had this visit while Rebecca and Jeff packed. The only thing on his mind right now was how she was going to react in her condition. He prayed she wouldn't lose the baby over this, she had been through enough as is and is concerned about how harmful this could be for her. That was when he realized he was falling in love with her. His feelings couldn't happen at a worse time. She still had to go through what was waiting for her at home. He would do anything to help her through this. Jeff went to bed with his head spinning, thinking about his feelings for her and worrying about her all t the same time. Now she has no one in her life to turn to. He had to be there for her and wanted to be there. He couldn't tell her how he felt; she was still getting over Wes. All he could do is put his feelings on the back burner for her until she was ready.

Rebecca was next door trying to rest, but was excited about going back home and seeing Paula. When she was shopping in town, she had found the cutest Mexican doll to remind her of their trip to the lodge and fiesta night. She bought something for Brad and Diane as well, and couldn't wait to give them their presents. There was a special one she just had to give right now. She went next door and knocked on Jeff's door. What a surprise to see her standing there.

"Is everything alright? Can I get you anything?"

"No, I'm fine. I was going to wait until I get back home, but I couldn't. I want to give this to you now. It's a thank you for helping me. I hope you like it, it's marble."

Jeff invited her in as he opened the package she gave him. It was a paperweight she bought him for his desk; in the middle was a brass coin shaped piece with his name inscribed.

"Thank you, but it really wasn't necessary."

"Not necessary? You helped save my life I think that's very necessary."

She leaned over and kissed him on the cheek and hugged him.

"I really did enjoy myself here. You have wonderful parents."

"They are special and they really like you. Well, I think we better get some rest for the trip back tomorrow. Thank you again and goodnight."

He showed her to the door and sat on his bed. She really is a wonderful woman. Any man would be pleased to have her in his life. Now that this would be over soon, maybe she would go out with him. There was something about her that really got under his skin. He really wanted to be with her, no matter what. The next day his parents drove them to the airport, wishing them a safe trip. Rebecca was holding her stomach as though something was about to happen.

"Jeff, look, she needs you."

They all rushed over to be with her.

"Are you alright? Are you in labor?"

"No, I'm not. I guess I thought I felt something, but I'm fine. We better board the plane, I don't want to miss this flight."

"Jeff, keep an eye on her, she may be ready sooner than either of you think."

"Don't worry, I'll look after her. I'll call you."

Mr. and Mrs. Fanala waited until they were on the plane before they left. Jeff called James to let him know they were on their way and warned them about Rebecca's condition. The flight was taking off and she was placid, Jeff put his hand on hers.

"Is everything alright?"

"I'm fine, just a little tired. I didn't really get much sleep last night."

"I know what you mean, I didn't either. Why don't you sit back and close your eyes and take a catnap? By the time we arrive in Arizona you'll be rested."

"That sounds great, I think I will. Thank you."

Almost instantly she was sleeping and all she could think about was home. While sleeping, she dreamed about Brad, Diane, and Paula, and all the good times they shared. Hopefully all the madness will be over with. Even Wes was in her dream; he stood in front of her talking to her.

"I wish I could be there with you and our baby, but that's not possible. You must really love me to go through everything you're going through right now, but baby, it's time you move on. I love you, but I want you to be happy, and you can't if you don't let me go and get on with your life. Take care of you and our baby, I'll always love you."

As the plane was landing, Rebecca was tossing in her seat. Jeff nudged her to wake her. When she sat up breathing heavily.

"What's wrong?"

"It's nothing, I was just dreaming."

She looked out the window and saw James waiting for them, but didn't see Paula. As soon as the passengers could leave their seats, Rebecca practically ran to get off the plane. Jeff was nearly running after her just to keep up.

"James, how are you? Where is Paula? Didn't she come with you?"

"She couldn't make it, let's get your luggage and we'll be on our way."

Jeff and James looked at each other, feeling apprehensive about this situation. James pulled the car around while Jeff and Rebecca collected the luggage. They packed up the car and were soon on their way. Something was wrong and she could feel it in her bones.

"I have to stop at a friend's house to pick up some papers, would either of you mind?"

"Not at all, it feels so good to be home again. I just want to enjoy it all."

"I would like to know what's going on? Something doesn't feel right and I would like to know right now. James, what is wrong?"

"I never could talk and drive at the same time. We're almost there, then we can talk."

He tried his best to stall her, but she was inpatient. This was not going to be easy.

Thirty minutes later, James pulled in Lewis's driveway, then beeped the horn to alert him they arrived.

"I'd like for you both to come in and meet Lewis. We're longtime friends and go back a long way."

As they approached the door to knock, Lewis opened it to greet his guests.

"Welcome home, please come in. We can use my office. Everything is ready, James. So, you must be Miss Travis, James has told me a little about you. I believe you're Jeff, welcome to my home. Let's all sit down."

James began the conversation, nervously and reluctantly.

"Rebecca, I'd like to start off by apologizing to you. We brought you here for a reason. Lewis is a friend of mine; he's also a psychiatrist. We all wanted to be here with you when we say what we have to tell you, and this won't be easy."

"What's going on, you're starting to scare me?"

Lewis abruptly joined in the conversation, since he better understood what was about to be said.

"We know what Paula means to you, but she's dead."

Standing up hysterically, she was getting excited.

"I wanted to be the one to explain things, because of my past history with Paula."

"What are you talking about?"

"This isn't easy, so I'll just get on with this. Years ago, she led a difficult life. I don't mean struggle, I mean abusive. Due to that life she dealt with, she started seeing me professionally."

"None of this makes sense. If this is true, why didn't she tell me?"

"Most likely she wouldn't because of developments caused by her abuse. Paula was sexually abused for three years by her stepfather. Finally, she couldn't deal with it anymore. That was when her second personality was born, Paul"

"What, you're crazy! She was as normal as I am right now."

"I'm sorry, I wish that were true, but it isn't. I have all her records here, it's not normal practice but you can read them over if you like. I was trying to help her control her other personality. See, when she first became Paul, it was to get revenge on her stepfather for abusing her the way he did. She couldn't take it anymore, so as Paul, she killed him with an ax."

"I don't believe you, any of you."

"I didn't believe it either, until he showed me the records, and even then I had my doubts. Until last night, she was about to kill Lewis when I shot her, only I didn't know it was her until I removed the ski mask."

"You see that was how she became Paul; it was the only way she could do this. As Paul she wore a ski mask, shoulder pads and even weights in the boots she wore."

Rebecca tried to take it all in but it all sounded so crazy. Even looking at the records couldn't convince her.

"Listen to them Rebecca. James and Lewis have no reason to lie to you."

"You knew about this? How long have you known, Jeff? Why didn't you tell me?"

"Please don't blame him, I ordered him not to tell. Because of your condition we all wanted to be here to tell you this. Besides, he didn't know until last night."

"That's right, just last night when James called me and if it's any consolation, I didn't believe it either."

"Paula was sexually abused, that had a bad effect on her. It would anyone. She had no idea what she was doing nor was she aware of her other personality. Her mental state of mind took control over her. She had no way of controlling that. At least not without help. An ugly side of her emerged to protect her, that was how she survived. The bad part of it all is that she took offense to any man she felt would harm her or her loved ones. Unfortunately, when Paul was killed so was Paula. This is why we all wanted to be here for you so we can help you through this."

"This is crazy, she never told me anything about being abused and we told each other everything. She would have told me that."

"I'm not saying you two were not close but that was something she never talked about. Paula felt embarrassed about what happened so she kept things to herself. If only she would have talked about, it things may have turned out differently for her."

"Rebecca, when Lewis told me about this, I too was skeptical. I'm not saying any of it made sense because it did but even still it just didn't seem possible."

"He's telling you the truth. I could tell James had his doubts about what I was saying to him and unless you work with this like I have, it is difficult to comprehend that any of this could be for real. I've had cases where a person has had more than two personalities, sometimes five. It can be frightening but no one has any control over this."

"Jeff, did you know anything about this?"

"Not this, I find it shocking. Although I have read about I, but being so close to a case like this is pretty astonishing."

"What you have to understand is she was abused for three years and she was scared for her life. He threatened to kill her if she didn't do as he asked."

"That is the most awful thing I've ever heard."

"Yes it is. After three years a part of her decided it was enough and if she didn't have the strength to defend herself the other part will. Her other personality was Paul. Paul was a strong man who could handle anything and would protect Paula. Kind of like a defense mechanism built in when she needed protection. I almost had her completely back but for whatever reason she stopped her sessions with me."

"Are you saying she could have killed me?"

"No not you, you were not a threat to her. She went after any man who posed a threat of any kind or seemed to be."

"I did some checking on Bill at the restaurant where he had dinner the night he was killed. He was there with another woman. Can you remember anything about the night Bill was killed?"

"We were out celebrating and I remember after she came back from the ladies' room she said she had a headache and wanted to go home."

"Take a look at this entry in this journal then tell me if it could have been possible."

James pointed out a section for her to read, it was plain to see she was stunned and couldn't believe what she was reading.

"Now do you remember Wes's death? Read this section here."

The handwriting was hers but the words were not. Rebecca was reading how she committed the murders and how she sneaked off to commit them. Wes was killed a day or two before they arrived back from their vacation. According to the journal she sneaked back to town in the rental in the middle of the night to kill him. By morning the car had cooled down and she was fixing breakfast. Paula had a lot of people fooled, even herself.

"I can let you read on but the remainder of everything written in here turns out the same. Look at the inside cover, it's inscribed Paul Devil. Her last name spelled backwards. Another sign of her split personality."

Rebecca didn't know how to respond. She wanted to cry but she couldn't. All she could feel was numb. What if she made Paula angry? Would she have gone after her? There was just no telling what could have been. It was spooky.

"I feel like an idiot. All this went on when I was with her! She seemed so sincere about losing Bill."

"She probably was. Paula was never aware of Paul, but her Paul side was totally aware of Paula."

She read over the files on both James and Lewis. One moment she felt bad for her until she read the journals. Rebecca was in tears just reading about how she was abused. It was hard to imagine even going through what Paula did. Right down to her mother leaving her with him. It couldn't have been easy for her mother to just leave her like that either. After so much reading she didn't want to read anymore and sat in the chair stunned, this was someone she was close to and spent time with.

"It's like someone I never knew!"

"As long as she was Paula she was safe to others. Remember the man who threatened you? Deep inside Paul knew you were in danger and was going to stop it before you were hurt. Paul didn't want anyone hurt like Paula was."

"This is all so ludicrous, and scary. I think understanding it makes it even scarier. What about my baby, why would she want to hurt my baby?"

"The baby was part of Wes and she considered Wes to be bad. Therefore, any part of Wes would have to be bad as well.

Momentarily she was thinking, then it hit her, Paula was gone.

"Oh Paula, why?"

Tears rolled down her face as Jeff tried to comfort her. James and Lewis were feeling terrible about this but she had to know. Then she looked up a brief moment.

"How did she die?"

"Why put yourself through any unnecessary heartache. It's over."

"I want to know; I need to know."

James reluctantly began to explain what happened. As she stood up to walk around and try to comprehend she felt a sudden pain to warn her the baby was arriving. Rebecca let out scream like she never had holding her stomach.

"Oh my God my baby. Jeff please help me."

"James, you're a cop. Weren't you trained for this?"

"Let me in there. We had better start timing her contractions."

James was showing Jeff how to help her breathe. He caught on quickly.

"Do you think all this brought on her contractions?"

"Who cares. Just please help me!"

James and Jeff tried to get her calmed down while Lewis called for an ambulance.

"They're on their way, about a few minutes."

The first set of contractions had stopped.

"She tried to kill you didn't she Lewis?"

"Don't think about that now, concentrate on your baby."

"I want to give birth with a clear mind and I can't do that without knowing. Please tell me."

"Yes she did. I'll get some sheets. Hang in there. You can do this."

That was the last question she had. Now she didn't have any more time to think of Paula. The next set of contractions began when the ambulance attendants arrived. Jeff was playing coach while James gave them all the information he could get. They checked her vital signs then prepped her for the delivery room.

"Jeff, please go with me."

"Are you sure you want me to go?"

As loud as she could, Rebecca shouted "yes." That was all he needed to hear. Then jumped in the back of the ambulance. He held her hand knowing he couldn't have been much comfort in her condition. She was having a baby.

"I want you to know, if there is any way I can be of help, I'll be there for you."

"That's sweet, now hold my damn hand and…aahhhh!"

He was beginning to find out the hard way that a woman having a baby tends to change her personality. This was a first for Jeff and he was learning firsthand about pain through birth. Yet in the end it would be a wonderful experience. The ambulance hit a few bumps but basically it was a smooth ride. Rebecca couldn't stop screaming and the contractions were getting closer and closer.

"Jeff, where are you?"

"I'm right here beside you, what can I do?"

"Please let me hold your hand, I feel another contraction."

She squeezed his hand so hard he thought it would fall off. Jeff tried to help her breathe but she was growing tired. He tried his best to keep her going and helped her with her breathing.

"Are we there yet? What is taking so long?"

"Relax we'll get there in plenty of time."

One of the attendants was taking her vital signs.

"We're almost there now, the nurses are waiting and the doctor is preparing for the birth. You're in good hands and everything will be fine."

"How would you know? Did you ever have a baby? You're just a want-to-be doctor."

"Rebecca, please."

"It's alright, all our mothers-to-be go through the same thing. She may never even remember what she says after this is all over with."

The ambulance pulled in and the nurses were waiting. As quickly as they could, they rushed her to the delivery room. One of the nurses helped Jeff scrub and prepare, him for the delivery.

"Wait, I'm not the father!"

"There is no time to waste. Scrub up now."

Things were so hectic the nurse didn't even hear what he had to say. Soon he was in the room with Rebecca. He was nervous, and again tried to tell the nurse he was not the father but no one would listen to him. They were all focused on Rebecca.

"Jeff, are you here?"

"Yes, here I am. You're going to be fine. Remember your breathing. Breathe in, then out."

"I can't do this. I'm tired. I want to sleep."

"I don't think you'll be sleeping through contractions."

"Then get this baby out of me.aahhh!"

The doctor came in and everyone was ready, especially Rebecca. He checked to see how close she was to delivering.

"It's alright, it will all be over soon. Looks like very soon. Are you ready?"

"Yes I'm ready. Can't you hurry?"

"Rebecca, I'm right here."

"Jeff, you're in the delivery room with me, I think you can call me Becki…"

"Oh God, my baby is coming. Now!"

"Ready, when I say take a deep breath, push. Here we go, push."

With all she had, she pushed as hard as she could. Jeff was doing a great job coaching her and never once left her side since this began.

"You're doing just fine. Stop and take a few breaths. When you're ready, take another deep breath and push."

"I'm pushing; how much longer will I have to wait?"

"One more should do it, ready? Push!"

A few short breaths, then one deep one, and she pushed. The doctor said all she needed was one more good push and it would all be over. So again she took a very deep breath and gave it all she had. Rebecca could feel the baby push all the way through. She leaned back to rest and breathe. It was all over. The doctor asked Jeff if he wanted to cut the cord, and he did. The nurses cleaned the baby and the doctor examined the newborn. The next sound in the room was the baby crying. Rebecca lay with perspiration pouring from her. Jeff wiped her face gently and thanked her for letting him be a part of this miracle.

"After all we've been through, I didn't see the harm in any of this. Thank you for being here with me."

"You did a great job. I'm proud to say you have a healthy baby girl."

"Do you hear that Becky; you have a daughter?"

"A baby girl? She is healthy. Right doctor?"

"Yes she is and she has a full head of hair."

The nurse brought her over to see her mother, Becki was so proud.

"She looks just like her mother."

"How can you tell? She's still so tiny, but she is beautiful. I have so much to share with you. I promise to take very good care of you."

She looked down at her daughter holding her close and talking to her as if she could understand what she was saying.

"So what do you think you'll name her?"

"I want to name her Madison, after my mother."

www.ingramcontent.com/pod-product-compliance
Lightning Source LLC
LaVergne TN
LVHW021238080526
838199LV00088B/4566